Searching for Sophia

A Novel by

Barbara Gerdau Drotar

Searching for Sophia

ISBN: 978-1-61170-210-1

Cover illustration by Dave O'Shea.

Published by:

Robertson Publishing™
www.RobertsonPublishing.com

Printed in the USA and UK on acid-free paper.
To purchase additional copies of this book go to:

    amazon.com
    barnesandnoble.com
    www.rp–author.com/drotar

DEDICATION

I thank my inspiring and loving husband, Dave,
and my amazing children and grandchildren,
who encouraged me to tell this story.

To My Dear Friend Audrey,
Barbara has been blessed
with the gift of writing
and I am so blessed to
be the recipient of that
gift. God bless you dear
friend.

Love you,

♡ Trish

Your friend forever!

"THE TRUE VALUE OF A HUMAN BEING IS DETERMINED
PRIMARILY BY THE MEASURE AND THE SENSE IN WHICH
HE HAS ATTAINED LIBERATION FROM SELF."

—ALBERT EINSTEIN (1879-1955)

CHAPTER ONE

JULY, 1993

At 10 o'clock each morning the black limousine drove through the white wrought iron gates leading to the ivy covered mansion. Dust rose through the air as it moved slowly up the mile-long gravel driveway, and pulled into one of only ten parking spaces in front. Lou Vindigni, the short, stocky, jut-jawed driver walked around to the passenger side rear door and opened it. Trent Martin stepped out of the back seat, looking older than his fifty-eight years. He slowly made his way up the stairs leading to the French doors. As soon as he entered the foyer, his demeanor changed as he greeted two young nurses in white, chatting behind a white marble desk.

"Good morning, ladies," Trent said with a smile.

"Good morning, Mister Martin," they replied in unison.

For the past eight months, Lou drove him from his home in San Francisco to visit his wife, Alexandra, at Casa de Madonna Convalescent Home, tucked away in the plush hills of Marin County. Daily, he wore a navy blue pin-striped suit, white starched shirt and a red tie to make the visits. At least one day a week he showed up with flowers and boxes of See's candy for the staff.

Alexandra was propped up with pillows on her bed. Her private nurse, Kristin, knew to leave the room as soon as Trent arrived, ensuring privacy for the husband and wife. Alexandra's room was decorated with pink and white rose-covered wall paper, white Irish lace curtains, and soft pink eyelet bedding. Although she looked paler than usual, the pink cashmere negligee she wore cast a soft blush on her cheeks. She stared at the curtains fluttering through the slightly opened window that summer morning. Trent hadn't seen his wife looking so radiant for a long time. He kissed her lips and each cheek. He hugged her. Just for a moment, he thought she recognized him.

Trent pulled the recliner close to the head of her bed to situate himself for another day. He gave into the cloak of fatigue that hit him often without warning, drifting into a restless sleep while attempting to eradicate the bitterness threatening to choke the life right out of him. Alexandra's enemy and thief was Alzheimer's disease. She was only fifty-three years old.

She began experiencing minimal memory loss five years earlier, which became increasingly frustrating for her. She kept the lapses to herself for as long as she could. Alex had no idea that Trent and their sixteen year old daughter, Sophia, shared their concerns about her. They watched her closely while her confusion increased at an alarming rate. If any of their relatives had noticed, no one said a word until a neurologist diagnosed her.

Trent began taking care of Alex full time after she walked out of their house six months earlier. Nothing seemed out of the ordinary. He was working at his law firm downtown, while Lou Vindigni, their housekeeper, cook and limousine driver, was busy doing chores in the Victorian estate. After lunch, Lou told Alexandra that he was going to run errands, and she told him that she might take a walk around the neighborhood while he was gone. She didn't care for working out at the club like most of her friends did, so she walked through their Pacific Heights neighborhood a few times a week to keep fit and clear her mind. It was 4:30 p.m. when Lou returned home. He was surprised to find Lou's neighbor, Frances Flori, sitting by herself on the couch in the living room.

"Is there something wrong?" Lou asked as he rushed through the door carrying grocery bags.

"Oh, thank God you're back. I didn't know what to do," she stuttered.

"What's going on...what is wrong...where is Alex?"

"She's fine now," Frances whispered, shaking her head. "She's upstairs in bed."

Lou pulled up one of the arm chairs closer to Frances. "This isn't an inquisition, but I'm losing patience here, what's going on?"

"Give me a chance to collect my thoughts, Lou. It was 2 o'clock when I left to go to the club for a swim. As soon as I turned onto Sacramento Street, I saw Alex sitting on the curb and hugging her purse tight against her chest. At first I couldn't believe it was her, she just didn't look like herself ... we've been best friends for twenty years. I swear on my father's grave she didn't know who I was. Can you imagine? We raised our children together."

Frances broke down in tears. Lou handed her his handkerchief. All he wanted to do was run up the stairs to see how Alex was, but he had to hear the rest of the story.

"She studied my face and our surroundings, and it was clear she recognized neither. I can't tell you how relieved I was when she finally remembered who I was, and asked why we were sitting on the curb. I told her we had been

3

taking a walk, and that we decided to sit down for a rest. She believed me. I drove her home. Alex had left the front door wide open, which as you know, is not like her at all. When I got her home all she wanted to do is go to bed, so I took her upstairs and she climbed under the covers with her clothes on.

Lou moved to sit down on the couch next to Frances, putting his arm around her shoulder. "Thank you. What can I say, if you hadn't picked her up who knows what could have happened?"

"I know she has been having a hard time remembering things, and hasn't been able to play Bridge with our club for about a year now, but I didn't realize she was getting so much worse." Frances got up and headed toward the front door. "I had better get going, Frank will be getting home any minute. If I don't have dinner on the table by 6 o'clock he turns into an ogre."

Lou opened the door for her. "Give my love to Trent. I don't know how he's going to handle this," she said, heading down the stairs.

"I know. And by the way, tell that husband of yours he'd better appreciate you. He doesn't know how good he has it."

"Oh, Lou, what will I do without her?" she said, wiping the tears from her cheeks.

Lou closed the door and went upstairs to peek in on Alexandra. She was sound asleep.

CHAPTER TWO

Getting lost that day changed everything. Trent quit going to work so he could stay home with Alex. With the new arrangement, both he and Lou could keep a closer eye on her. It gave the couple much needed time together, if only to talk and play board games, at least when she could still participate.

One year later, Alexandra got out of bed in the middle of the night and went downstairs to the kitchen. When the smoke-detector went off, both men ran down the stairs to find a flaming pan on the gas burner, full of burnt scrambled eggs stuck to the bottom. They found her asleep on Trent's recliner in the library. After that night, he and Alexandra began sleeping in separate bedrooms and he started locking her door from the outside after she went to sleep.

The neurologist suggested that Trent find a convalescent home that could provide around-the-clock nursing care for her. Alex's mental, physical and emotional states were declining rapidly. Without provocation, she would scream at him, sometimes even punching him in the face. He knew it was the disease, not his wife, never the less the heartache it caused had become unbearable.

Trent and their daughter, Sophia, then twenty-one, spent a few weeks visiting homes specializing

5

in Alzheimer's patient care. He was relieved that Sophia was doing so well since coming out of a rehab facility two months earlier; the third program she had been through. When she was sixteen years old, shortly after her mother was diagnosed with the horrible disease, she started using drugs. She was a big help to Trent in their search for the best residence for Alexandra's care. It was an exhausting exercise, while moving toward the inevitable.

Seemingly out of the blue, Sophia started refusing to go with him to check out facilities for her mother. The girl was changing. She began spewing hateful things like, "I'm not going to anymore of those nut houses with you, Dad. They make me want to puke! They all smell like piss!"

Trent felt guilty for being so relieved when she stopped going with him. It was obvious she was relapsing, which was breaking his heart, knowing he was powerless to help her. His very limited reserve of energy needed to be used for his wife.

Driving Alexandra to Casa de Madonna Convalescent Home was the most devastating day of Trent's life. He felt like he was playing a dirty trick on her, like a parent taking his child to an orphanage.

Lou would take long walks around the beautifully landscaped acreage surrounding Casa de Madonna while Trent sat with his wife. He had been working for the Martin family since Sophia was six years old. Lou never had a family of his own, so watching Trent's family falling apart hit him hard. He loved Alexandra like a sister, his boss like a brother and Sophia like a niece.

Before the sun set every day, the men drove over the Golden Gate Bridge on their way back home. It was a grueling trip after long hours spent with Alex, and Trent didn't want to miss one chance to catch her being herself, but he desperately needed to sleep in his own bed so the trips were necessary.

On a Tuesday morning, Trent broke.

CHAPTER THREE

Alexandra started to thrash around in her bed. Her arms flailed and her fists clenched like she was boxing a demon only she could see. Her agitation seemed to increase daily, some worse than others. Trent had learned to soothe her with an exercise he thought up months before. He reached over to the side table where he kept the boxes of pink tissue, carried her out of bed and placed her in a chair that could be adjusted to a semi-sitting position, and tucked pillows around her to prevent flopping to either side. Since the first day he wiped her mouth with a piece of the pink tissue, Alex appeared to perk up a bit. He figured it might be his imagination playing tricks on him, but he was sure it was the pink of the tissue that she reacted favorably to.

He handed her one piece of tissue at a time, and she carefully folded it twice, making four perfect squares. As soon as she began the repetitive exercise, she settled down. She folded tissue after tissue, making neat stacks on a table next to the chair. She usually stayed on task for about fifteen minutes before dozing off. Trent had just handed his wife another piece of tissue to add to her carefully stacked pile. He hadn't noticed Sophia had entered the room until it was too late.

"Dad!" she screamed. "Why are you wasting your

time? She doesn't even know who you are!"

Trent pushed his chair back in an attempt to stop his daughter as she grabbed the piles of folded tissue off the table and threw them at her mother's face. She leaned in close to Alexandra, mocking her and hysterically laughing. "Who the hell am I, Mama?"

He wrestled his drugged-up daughter off Alex and threw her to the floor. The nightmare was happening fast. Sophia's greasy-haired, tattooed boyfriend with missing front teeth rushed into the room.

"Leave her alone, you fucking idiot!" he yelled, wild-eyed.

Trent slammed the derelict against the wall as Sophia grabbed her father's ankle with both hands. He struggled to kick her off, dragging her around the room. He had never even yelled at his own flesh and blood before. He yelled for Security.

Sophia writhed as a security guard pulled her off her father. The police arrived within five minutes. She and her boyfriend were handcuffed and taken outside. Trent, stunned, watched through the window as Sophia was stuffed into the back seat of a squad car and driven away. Catching sight of the police driving away, Lou rushed back to Alexandra's room. Trent stood in the middle of the room, sobbing. He had never seen his boss like this before.

"I've lost them both!"

"It's the drugs, Boss. You will get your daughter back, I promise."

"My wife...my daughter...my God, where the hell are they?" Trent's voice sounded like it was coming from a deep abyss.

Slumped in the chair, Alexandra had slept through it all.

Trent called his friend and San Francisco Police Chief, Rob Becker, the afternoon after Sophia's arrest. Becker told him that she had been released from jail early that morning. As a personal favor, Rob agreed to put an all-points bulletin out. Every cop on every beat throughout Northern California was alerted to keep an eye out for her.

Unlike other times Sophia ran away while under the influence, this time she didn't call her dad. Four weeks after not hearing one word from her, Trent met with Vernon Rush, a private investigator who had worked with Lou years before. He was impressed with the P.I.'s no-nonsense demeanor, and with Lou's glowing recommendation, he was hired. In their agreement it was stipulated that Trent would receive daily reports concerning any leads to Sophia's whereabouts. He wrote up a contract that any P.I. in the country would have fought hard to get.

CHAPTER FOUR

A couple of months passed without any news on Sophia. Some nights after returning from Marin County, Trent would walk the streets alone in a daze, aimlessly searching for her. Alexandra was losing her appetite and was having a hard time eating solid food. Sometimes she chewed on a piece of meat, but forgot to swallow or how to swallow, it was hard to tell which. His stress level was sucking the life right out of him. During a weekly conference with Alex's neurologist, Trent was told that her life expectancy was three to six months.

"You know what," Lou said, driving home one night, "people from all over the world come here just to catch a glimpse of this bridge and our beautiful skyline. We take it for granted."

"We sure do," Trent agreed, leaning forward to get a fuller view of the sky's radiant hues of reds and yellows. A cassette tape playing Glenn Miller's music soothed their nerves during the trip home every night.

"Look out!"

Sirens screamed, lights flashed and helicopters circled overhead when Lou opened his eyes. Paramedics were carrying him on a stretcher, jerking it while pushing him through the back doors of an ambulance. He couldn't find his bearings as he slid in and out of consciousness. The last thing he saw as he craned his head back were the Jaws of Life ripping the back door off the limousine, before passing out again.

"Where the hell is my boss?" Lou whispered, struggling to push himself off a gurney in the emergency department of a hospital. He was hooked up to an IV; pain seared through every inch of his body.

"Settle down, Mr. Vindigni. You are at San Francisco General Hospital," a nurse slowly focused through his blurred vision and muffled hearing. "You were involved in an accident. Don't move or you will injure yourself more," she said, firmly holding his shoulders down on the gurney.

Tears rolled down his cheeks. "Where is my boss, is he okay?"

"Mister Martin is in surgery right now. Our best orthopedic surgeons are working on him. Listen, some of your ribs are broken and the doctors are keeping a close eye on your spleen, so you need to stay calm and quiet, understand? I am going to increase the pain medication through your I.V.," she said, increasing the dose. "You'll go to sleep now."

It was still dark when Lou woke up in a hospital room. He pushed the call button and a nurse came in. She reported that Trent had made it through surgery for a fractured hip, broken femur and a dislocated shoulder, explaining that his surgery went well, but he would need to be hospitalized for a couple of weeks before needing further recovery at a rehabilitation facility. She went on to tell Lou that if there were no complications in his case, he could be released from the hospital in a few days.

"You don't understand, Trent has to get out of here. His wife is dying. He will come apart without her. Please..." The pain medication dripping through his I.V. put him back to sleep.

Lou was having a difficult time waking up when he heard voices calling his name.

"Mr. Vindigni ... Mr. Vindigni ... wake up, sir." Two police officers were sitting on chairs close to Lou's bed.

He woke up startled, seeing them next to him, clipboards poised on their laps.

"What did I do?" he strained to ask.

"You're not in any trouble," one of the officers assured Lou. "We need to ask you a couple of questions. Do you remember the accident?"

"No."

"You didn't do anything wrong," the officer on his right continued. "A truck rolled over at the west end of the Golden Gate Bridge. Eight vehicles were involved in the pileup. Are you up to hearing this right now? We don't want to upset you."

"Did I cause the accident?"

"No, you didn't. Yours was the fifth vehicle in the pileup. So, you don't remember anything?"

"No, I don't. It was such a beautiful sunset...a real pretty one, you know?"

"We know. We'll be leaving now, you'd better get some rest. If you have any questions," officer Ray Janakes said, reaching into his breast pocket, "here's my card."

The policemen left the room. Later that afternoon Lou received a phone call from a representative at San Francisco City Hall checking on how he and Trent were doing.

CHAPTER FIVE

The following month was agonizing. Trent suffered through physical therapy in the hospital, and was later sent to a rehabilitation center for further strength-building. Being separated from Alexandra was torture.

Trent never could tolerate the sights and smells of sickness. The rehab center catered to accident and stroke victims, some as young as eighteen years of age. Wrenching sounds of stroke victims struggling to learn how to swallow and speak, made him gag. He had an orderly push him into a small garden area outside so he could avoid the noise blaring from the television in the recreation room. The sight of wheel chairs lined up, while blank-faced patients watched soap operas, ground his nerves. When patients pounded on the piano, he had to be removed from the area.

On the phone one night, he told Lou, "If I have to look at one more biker-dude with stumps for legs, I will throw myself out this damn window. I can't take this pressure much longer."

"You'll be out of there soon. Just do the work so you can get back to Alex. She's holding on for you."

Since his release from the hospital, Lou and Alex's mother took turns visiting her every day. Lou had been released from the hospital three days after the accident, but continued to suffer pain while his ribs were healing, so the trip to and from Marin County was arduous and exhausting. He called Trent every night to give a report on Alex, always giving a positive spin on her condition. The truth was, she was existing on small amounts of baby food and sips of water.

Trent became physically and psychologically stronger as he made progress towards the day he could leave the rehabilitation center. As soon as he could use a walker, he was released. Lou drove him to see Alexandra the same day. He was stunned by how poorly she was doing, but the joy of being able to hold her in his arms seemed to lessen the pain.

A week later, Trent had just returned from a short walk around the grounds and went into the bathroom in Alex's room.

"Mister Martin?" the nurse called for the third time, "are you all right?"

"I'm fine, Kristin," he answered not quite sounding like himself.

She knew that he frequently locked himself in the bathroom, privately crying for his daughter. He talked a lot about Sophia with Kristin, saying that sometimes he couldn't take a breath, not knowing if he would ever see the apple of his eye again. Trent and his daughter had had the close bond that most dads only dream of. The man was being torn in two…literally.

"I thought you were off at 3 o'clock," Trent said, glancing at his watch when he came out of the bathroom, wiping his nose with tissue.

"I do, but I waited for you to come back. Can I ask you a question?"

"Of course you can, take a seat. Before you ask, I don't think I have ever really told you how much I appreciate the wonderful way you take care of my wife."

"It has been an honor, Mister Martin. I am the one who wants to thank you."

"For what?"

"For giving me hope. I have worked here for six years, but I have never seen anyone give love like you give Mrs. Martin. You would be shocked to see some of the things I've seen around here: husbands, wives, and family members treating my patients with neglect and cruelty. It would make you sick to your stomach. Most of the time they don't get any visitors. Thank you for giving me hope that somewhere in this world there could be a man who would love me unconditionally like you love your wife."

"Thank you, Kristin, but if you really knew Alex, you would know that I am the lucky one. Just know that any man worth his salt will love you the way you deserve."

"Is it okay if I ask how you and Mrs. Martin met?"

"I haven't thought about that night for a long time. This is going back twenty-seven years, but I'd enjoy telling you. Let's see, I had made last minute plans to attend a charity ball at the Fairmont Hotel. Standing around with some of my friends at one of the hors d'oeuvre bars in the lobby, I turned around so abruptly that I caused a young woman to fall down, making quite a scene. We didn't have a chance to take a good look at each other because we quickly got down on our knees to pick up the food we dropped."

As Trent told the story, he smiled, coming alive like Kristin had never seen him before. He appeared years younger while he reminisced.

"I helped her to her feet, and we both burst out

16

laughing, then I took a good look at her and almost lost my breath. She was stunning. Alexandra Rose Lombardi was the most beautiful woman I had ever seen. It took me about 5 seconds to recognize that she wasn't just another debutante princess, she actually had a sense of humor about my clumsiness. While she wiped some food off her dress, I took the opportunity to look her over," Trent smiled. "She had the most beautiful long auburn hair and a pair of legs that could kill. I'd better keep this G-rated," he said with a twinkle in his eye.

"Don't leave me hanging here, what happened next?" Kristin asked, sitting on the edge of her seat.

"We had barely said a few words when the head of the Banquets Department announced that dinner was being served in the ballroom. Hundreds of men and women started walking out of the reception area. One of Alex's friends rushed up to her, tugged on her arm, saying it was time to go to their table. Alex told her to go ahead, and that she would catch up later. I told Alex that I found those events boring, and asked if she would like to have dinner with me downstairs in the Tonga Room. I couldn't believe it when she said yes. She caught up to her friend to fill her in, and we left. She made it very clear that she wasn't used to taking off with someone she didn't know, but as long as she was back to her friend's table by 1 a.m. she would make an exception. To tell you the truth, and not to brag, I was used to getting any girl I wanted. But I hadn't felt that light-hearted since the prettiest girl in 6th grade said hi to me for the first time. This has to be boring you."

"Not at all."

"Okay, I must admit I'm enjoying telling you. Alex had attended other functions at the Fairmont before, but she had never been to the Tonga Room downstairs. When we entered the room, she said she felt like we had traveled to a Polynesian island."

"Some of my friends have been there, what is it like?"

"Torches burn throughout the dining room, surrounded by palm trees. Large buffet tables, covered with canopies, resemble grass huts. That night a four-piece band played soft music, and a mock rainstorm with occasional thunder booming felt magical. I had dined there many times before, but I saw everything like it was my first time. The hostess seated us at a corner table. From the moment we sat down, the natural exuberance and intimacy of our connecting was palpable."

"How old were you when you guys met?"

"She was twenty-six and I was thirty-one. She had just graduated from U.C.S.F.'s School of Nursing. She worked in the I.C.U. department at the medical center, working with kidney-transplant patients. I was deeply moved as I listened to her love and dedication for her patients. I kept asking her questions while we ate dinner, which was unusual because I usually did all of the talking on dates," he grinned.

"Did she live in the city too?"

"Yes, she lived in North Beach with her best friend, Bev, who was a stewardess.

"Did you guys hit it off right away?"

"We sure did, and the great thing was that she clearly had never heard of me before that night. It wasn't until we were eating dessert that I gave her a chance to ask me questions about myself. Usually, women only showed interest in me for my notoriety and wealth. When we were slow-dancing after dessert, I knew that one day she would be my wife. One year later we were married. It was the happiest day of my life." Trent reached over for tissue and wiped his eyes.

"Thank you, Mister Martin. That was a beautiful story," Kristin said, as she took a piece of the tissue, wiping her eyes. "I hope Sophia comes back to you soon," she whispered as she left the room.

Trent was able to be with Alexandra the last two weeks of her life. When she took her last breath, he slammed his walker against the wall.

CHAPTER SIX

The funeral Mass was held at Saints Peter and Paul Catholic Church in North Beach. Alex was baptized there as an infant, received her First Communion at seven years old, confirmed at twelve, and married Trent when she was twenty-seven. They raised Sophia in the same close-knit church community.

Twenty-seven years earlier, Alex processed up the aisle on her father's arm to get married, she was now being carried in a casket. Trent walked in front of her while six pallbearers carried her to the altar. *Ave Maria*, her favorite hymn, was played on the hundred-year-old pipe organ during the procession up the aisle. The church was packed.

The mass was celebrated by four priests who knew the family well. The main celebrant was 92-year-old Father Raphael Cervantes, who had been priest, confessor and close friend to three generations of the Lombardi family. Both mourning and celebration took place as family, friends, and city officials took turns speaking from the pulpit. One after the next shared beautiful and often humorous ways Alex impacted their lives. Her passing at such a young age, felt like a dire offense against nature.

After mass, Trent sat in the front seat of the white hearse carrying Alex's remains to the cemetery. Their families filled two black hearses that followed. The city of San Francisco provided a motorcycle police escort for the three miles of cars driving in solemn procession to Holy Cross Cemetery in Colma where Alex's coffin would be placed in the Lombardi family mausoleum.

At the gravesite, Father Cervantes read some final prayers before inviting everyone to take one of the hundreds of white roses blanketing her coffin. Trent went up first. One of Alex's brothers had to finally pull him away and help him back to the hearse. Trent collapsed, wailing.

In eerie quiet, family and friends filed up to take a rose, as though the flower was a part of Alex they could take home with them. In silence, everyone left the cemetery.

CHAPTER SEVEN

L ou opened the door to Trent's bedroom, laid a break-fast tray on his bedside table, and yanked the drapes open.

"Hey, wake up," Lou repeated for the third time with no response from Trent.

Pulling the covers up over his face, Trent dismissed Lou with a flip of his hand.

"Just leave the tray on the table, I'm not getting up yet," he whispered in a raspy voice. He rolled away from the window, telling Lou to shut the damn drapes.

"I will not!" Lou shouted. "You see this food? You want me to cook for you anymore? You will have to come down to the dining room or you can damn well starve in here as far as I'm concerned." Lou picked up the tray and left the room.

He was downstairs in the pantry cutting herbs and potting an orchid, when he heard Trent coming down the stairs.

At the entrance to the pantry, Trent quipped, "Where the hell is my breakfast? You said it would be in the dining room."

Lou took his gardening gloves and apron off, and

turned around to see Trent, wearing his loosely-tied terry cloth robe, looking like a slovenly old man. He hadn't showered or shaved since his wife's funeral two weeks earlier.

"You think I'm your slave or something? I've got news for you, Boss," Lou shouted, pointing his finger at Trent. "I have worked for you and your family for sixteen years, but things are about to change. You want me to cook your meals, then show up in the dining room when I say so. If you're not on time, I'll just eat and do the dishes. Once the kitchen is clean, it's closed. I won't stand by and watch you make yourself sick. And, to honor your beloved wife, dress up for meals from now on. I'm so done with this crap."

Lou turned away, put his gardening gloves back on and resumed potting the plant. After a few minutes he wiped his drenched forehead with the back of his arm, and turned around. Trent had left the room.

CHAPTER EIGHT

Trent and Lou sat with 150 other passengers in the Maui Airport terminal waiting to board a flight back to San Francisco. It had been three months since Alexandra's funeral and Sophia hadn't been seen or heard from in six months. The trip to Maui was supposed to give Trent some relief. It hadn't.

Trent and Alex had vacationed on Maui every year of their marriage ... until she became ill. They loved the island, and because they were always over-extended with involvement in business and charitable events back home, their time in Maui gave them a chance to reconnect. They didn't like leaving Sophia at home while she was growing up, but they knew that their time alone was vital. Alexandra's mother stayed in their home to take care of Sophia during those getaways. Before the sunset every night, they telephoned her. Everywhere else they traveled, the family went together, but not Maui.

Trent and Lou planned on staying at Trent's condo for three weeks, but after two days Trent wanted to fly back home. He couldn't bear the flood of memories, especially the brilliant hues of color the sunsets displayed. He and Alex loved to sit on foldup chairs just feet from the Pacific Ocean and hold hands while watching the last sliver of sun disappear behind the island of Lanai.

Lou brought Trent a cup of coffee from one of the concessions in the terminal. Among those waiting to board was the Stanford University basketball team, who had just won the Maui Invitational, defeating Duke's Blue Devils 89-85 in double overtime. The athletes, wearing their Cardinal sweats, were ecstatic; the coaches were doing a great job of keeping them in check.

Boarding began, but because Trent had made the last-minute reservations, seats weren't available together. Lou sat near the back of the plane. While the jet taxied out to the runway and the flight attendant reviewed the emergency instructions, Trent laid his head against the headrest, trying to unwind. They took off, and as soon as the seatbelt sign went off, the athletes began walking around the plane.

The flight attendants served beverages, sandwiches and salads for dinner. Trent was eating a club sandwich with a soft drink, feeling strength returning to his mind and body. The trip had been physically and emotionally taxing.

"Excuse me," the flight attendant spoke over Trent, "would you like to order some dinner?"

"No thank you."

"Are you sure? It's going to be a five hour flight, and this will be the only meal service," she repeated.

"I'm fine," the young man answered.

Trent hadn't taken much notice of who was seated next to him, but he figured it was going to be a miserably long trip for the kid. The basketball player looked to be about 6 feet 8 inches tall, and about 250 pounds. Trent's legs were already beginning to cramp, but he was nowhere as tall as the basketball player. He noticed that the kid didn't eat or socialize with his teammates, nor did he put earphones on when the movie began.

"Hey, Stanford, are your earphones working?" Trent broke the silence, half joking.

"I don't know," he answered, not looking at Trent.

Trent tried to ignore the punk's attitude. "Congratulations on your win against Duke. I've always been a big Stanford fan. What position do you play?"

"Power Forward. I'm going to be sick!" He slammed his tray table closed, stumbled over Trent's legs and rushed up the aisle to the lavatory, snapping the occupied lock shut.

After watching the movie for fifteen minutes or so, Trent got concerned about the kid who was still in the lavatory. He was just about to get out of his seat to go check, when the door opened and the stone-faced young man returned, excusing himself as he climbed over Trent's legs to get back to his seat.

"Are you feeling okay? The flight attendant could get you a 7-Up or something," Trent suggested. He didn't respond. "It's going to be a long flight. My name is Trent Martin. What's yours?"

"David James. I'm fine."

Trent lost all desire to watch the movie, so he folded his earphones in the pocket in back of the seat in front of him. The two men stared straight ahead as if there was something to look at.

Trent started thinking about his daughter. David had to be about the same age, but he had a great future ahead of him. Sophia could be dead for all he knew. *What the hell, does this kid know how good he has it?*

Crossing his legs away from the darkness emanating from the moody basketball player, Trent got up and

26

walked to the back of the plane. Waking Lou from a deep sleep, he asked if he could trade seats because he didn't want to sit next to David anymore. Lou turned down the offer, pulling the bill of his baseball cap down over his eyes and fell back to sleep.

Trent made his way back up the center aisle, crowded with the Stanford athletes milling around. The rest of the flight was spent in silence. When a flight attendant offered David a second chance to get a sandwich, he turned away.

Trent pushed the call button to get the flight attendant's attention.

"I'll take that sandwich, if you don't mind," he said, taking it out of her hand. "Thank you very much."

"That's my sandwich," David said, seeming alert for the first time.

"Oh, now you want it, huh? If you say please, I guess I can give you half."

"Fine … please," he whispered.

He gave David the whole sandwich. David spent the rest of the trip trying to get comfortable in his seat, making Trent even more uncomfortable.

When they landed in San Francisco, the terminal was filled with family members and Stanford fans waving banners, balloons, and throwing red and white confetti on the players as they exited the plane. Members of the school's marching band, and the cheerleading squad formed an aisle for the players to walk through while everyone sang their fight song.

When David came out of the plane, he stopped for a second and touched Trent's shoulder. "Nice meeting you, Mister Martin," and continued to follow his team-mates.

After enjoying the fanfare, everyone walked toward

the baggage claim area down the escalator. Lou told Trent that he would go get their limousine and return to pick him up in front of Flight Arrivals. Trent caught sight of David sitting alone on a bench across from the baggage carousel. He was motionless, hunched over with his head hanging between his knees. His duffle bag hung from his folded hands outstretched in front of him.

Trent stood close by just looking at David, who appeared deep in thought, or lack of it. It was hard to tell which. He started to walk away toward the carousel, but felt himself being drawn back to David.

"Are you all right?" Trent asked, lightly poking his shoulder.

David jerked as if he had been somewhere else. He looked at Trent from a dark and empty space, as Trent sat down beside him.

"I don't mean to pry, but you look troubled."

"I'm fine. I just need to think," David whispered, shaking his head side to side. "I can't stand it anymore." Trent strained to hear what he was saying.

"What's the matter, son?" Trent was shocked at his choice of the word...son.

Tears puddled in David's eyes.

"My mother, little brother and sister could be dying while I'm having a good old time playing basketball and going to school."

Trent handed David his handkerchief.

"What the heck is going on here, Boss?" Lou asked in an accusatory tone, standing over the two men. "We have to get going, it's after midnight."

"I'd like to introduce you to Lou Vindigni. And Lou, this is David James. This is the kid I sat next to on the plane. As you can see, we are having a conversation. I think our luggage is ready on the carousel, I will meet you outside when we are finished talking. Thank you, Lou," Trent said, gritting his teeth.

Lou shook his head as he walked toward the luggage going around in circles.

———

"Start at the beginning. What's going on with your family?" Trent asked as if they hadn't been interrupted.

"You have to believe me, Mister Martin, my mother is the greatest woman in the world. A year ago, my stepfather left her and my brother and sister...just like that, the crazy drunk. Two months later Mama was evicted from her apartment. My family is living on the streets. They're cold and hungry, and maybe they're dead. I haven't seen them for two weeks, and they looked real sick and then I had to leave them to go back to school. I have another frigging year left of my scholarship, but I want to quit school and get a job to take care of my family. Mama cries when I tell her I'm going to quit school. She says it will kill her if I quit."

"All right, slow down and take a couple of deep breaths. Do you know where they are?"

"They're somewhere in Oakland. My brother is five, my sister is four, and Mama is thirty-seven, but she's skinny and she looks old like she's sixty or something. They move street to street with their belongings in a grocery basket. I found her digging for food out of a garbage can once, looking like she would fall right in. God, I hate myself!" David's eyes looked hollow and terror-filled as he spoke directly to Trent's gut.

"Maybe Mama's dead and the babies are lost and..."

Trent put his hand on David's shoulder, in an effort to

settle him down.

"Do you have to get back to school tomorrow?"

"No, we go back day after tomorrow."

"So you won't have to go back to school until Tuesday, right? Listen to me carefully. Look at me. I am going to help you find your family."

CHAPTER NINE

D avid followed him outside to the limousine parked in front of the terminal. After Trent explained the situation to Lou, the men headed toward the Bay Bridge on their way to Oakland.

"Do you remember where you last saw them?" Trent asked.

"They were living in a park somewhere near downtown. Another time they were sleeping behind a garbage bin in one of the industrial areas."

"Hey, David," Lou remarked, looking through the rearview mirror, "I used to be a private investigator, we'll find your family."

David slumped down, staring out the side rear window.

Lou continued, "When we get off the bridge I need you to show me exactly where you saw them last."

Lou made a right turn into a dark quiet area of Oakland. Industrial areas and alleyways blended together in the early morning hours. David's confusion heightened as they turned down street after street.

Poking Lou's shoulder, he shouted, "Stop here, this looks familiar...right here!"

Lou pulled over to the curb and turned off the engine.

"Why don't you wait here while David and I search a few streets at a time," Trent suggested. If we don't find them around here, we'll come back and head to another area. Does that work for you?"

"I agree. I'll wait right here. I'm sure you will find your family, David. Just get going."

———◦———

Lou locked the doors and pulled a loaded gun out of the glove compartment.

———◦———

Trent and David walked through streets and alleys, checking under dirty blankets and cardboard shacks. The city that appeared to be asleep was awake with wide-eyed fear staring back at them as they walked carefully past the homeless. It was unsettling as they dodged empty bottles of booze, discarded food wrappings, circling newspapers in windy alleyways, the pungent smells of streets without sanitary facilities and garbage cans without lids. The stench of unbathed humanity was nauseating. It tore at Trent's heart to realize that David's family could be found under the next layer of anything.

"Listen up," Trent broke the silence, "when we find your family, I promise, they will never be homeless again." David kept walking.

Trent began to panic when the image of Sophia's face flashed before his eyes. He was hit with the choking fear that his daughter might be homeless or worse, so he reined his mind away from the tormenting thoughts consuming him. He had always lived under the illusion that he was in charge of his and his family's destiny. Now he found himself without a family, rummaging through garbage with a young man he had met only hours before, to help a family he had never met, and might never meet.

After a fruitless hour of searching, the men returned to Lou. The temperature had dropped to 30 degrees so Lou had picked up cups of hot coffee and donuts for them. After warming up a bit, he drove them to another area.

After walking a few blocks, Trent and David entered streets that were pitch black. Shadows cast by tall commercial buildings, and an uninhabited paint-chipped hotel with cardboard taped over window frames blocked the moon's light. Without warning, David took off running ahead of Trent, and disappeared from sight.

"David, where are you? Wait for me!" Trent yelled, running down the middle of a dark alley, scanning side to side like a blind man.

"Oh my God! Mama, Mama," David shouted from somewhere in the dark, sounding like a lost ten year old boy. Straining to see in the dark, Trent froze when he caught sight of David draped over his family on the cold pavement. He was rocking them in his arms. Three pairs of hands were patting his back, like angels' wings fluttering.

Everything went quiet.

"Everybody, stay here…don't move, I'll be right back," Trent shouted over his shoulder, as he ran back up the middle of the street. Trent could hear the mother sobbing, "My son my son," sounding like a lullaby.

Trent banged on the limousine window, startling Lou, which was foolish since he had the loaded gun in his hand.

"What the hell?" Lou shouted through the closed window.

"We found David's family, they're just a few blocks away."

33

Within a couple of minutes they reached the alley. David was walking towards them, waving his arms like he was guiding in a jumbo jet.

The men got out of the car and followed David back to his family. His mother stood leaning against a wall at the farthest end of the alley and her small children stood motionless with their arms wrapped tightly around her legs. As soon as the woman saw the two strangers approaching her, she collapsed to the street. David sat down next to her and rocked his family, who were shivering so much their teeth could be heard clicking. The disheveled boy and girl stared up at their big brother from under their mother's arms while Trent rushed to get a couple of blankets out of the trunk. In an effort to curb the chill, he began to pat the blankets snug around the children. He stopped when noticing their bodies felt skeletal against his hands and was overcome with the sad thought of how easily they could break.

"Mama," David whispered, "I want to introduce you to two wonderful men. I met them on the flight back from Maui. They drove me here to find you."

Trent reached down to shake the mother's hand.

"It is nice to meet you, Ma'am. My name is Trent Martin. What is yours?"

"Dolores James," she answered not lifting her eyes. "This is Briana, and my son Matthew. Say hello to Mister Martin, children." The children buried their faces against their mother's chest. "God bless you for bringing David to us, I thought we were going to die," she whispered, hoping her children didn't hear.

"Where are my manners," David interrupted. "Mama, I want to introduce you to Lou." Lou shook her hand.

"Everything is going to be fine," Lou assured the young

mother. "We're going to get you out of this place."

"I don't know how to thank you gentlemen," she whispered, tears running down her sunken cheeks.

"Like he said, we are going to get you out of here, and there's no time like the present," Trent said, eyeballing David.

"But where are you taking us?" she asked, hugging the children tighter. "David, are you coming with us? We don't even know these men, maybe we should just stay put."

"I won't let you and the babies go anywhere without me, Mama."

"We can figure out somewhere safe and warm to go, but first, let's pick up your belongings," Trent said, attempting to reassure the family and convince himself.

It only took a few minutes to put everything into the trunk. Ripping up the large cardboard box the family had been living in, Trent and Lou both gagged as they stuffed the junk into a stinking dumpster.

"Just smell this crap," Trent grimaced through clenched teeth.

"Try not to blow a gasket, so where are we taking them?"

"Let's grab some food on the way home and we'll figure something out."

CHAPTER TEN

D avid sat with his family in the back seat of the limo. Dolores and the children fell asleep before they reached the bridge. Lou pulled up to Mel's Diner on Van Ness Avenue. Although it was just 6 a.m. when they walked into the diner that Monday morning, the place was packed. Dolores felt embarrassed when she noticed some of the diners staring at her and her children with disgust. She kept her eyes down, attempting to ignore the glares. Every chance she got, she slicked her matted hair back, trying to disguise the fact that she was using saliva to do the job. The hostess escorted the party of six to a large booth near the back of the restaurant. Slipping her a fifty dollar bill, Trent asked the hostess to hold their table while they all used the restrooms. The stress that had consumed the men since they left for Oakland had masked the fact that their bladders were about to burst.

Dolores took her children into the ladies room where she did her best to clean their hands, faces and hair with soapy paper towels. She looked in the mirror and got angry at herself for doing so. Living on the streets had afforded her a denial the mirror tore away.

———⁕———

David whispered through the restroom door. "Mama, hurry up, it's time to eat."

Dolores opened the door and came out with the children who still held onto her legs, being jerked with each step she took. Trent had taken liberty to order breakfast for everyone. The busboy pulled a small table close to the booth to accommodate the platters of food. She and the children weren't able to eat much. The men ate like there was no tomorrow.

"What do you think you are doing, young man?" Dolores whispered to her five year old. "What are you stuffing in your pockets? Take it out right now," she whispered, tugging Matthew's hands out of his sweatshirt pockets. The child wrestled his mother off, as she pulled scrunched-up napkins out of his pockets, which then unrolled across the table, leaving a trail of scrambled eggs and crumbled muffins landing on the floor. Trent and Lou drummed up conversation with David to draw focus away from what was going on, they didn't want to embarrass the child or Dolores more than they already were. Briana squeezed her eyes closed and covered her ears with her small dimpled hands.

"Mama, we'll be hungry tonight, don't throw the food away," the little guy begged while he crawled under the table, attempting to scoop the food back up with his hands. David reached under the table and lifted his brother back up to the booth. Sobbing, Matthew could barely breathe, while hiding his face into his mother's breast. She tried to console him while wiping away her own tears. For too long, the five year old had taken on the role as man of the family.

"Matthew," David whispered, "it will be okay. I love you, you're a good boy," he said, patting his little brother's shoulder.

Trent reached into his blazer pocket to answer his cell phone. "Hello...Vern? Wait a minute, it's too loud in here," he shouted, "I'll go outside...hold on." He rushed out of the restaurant to take the call.

Moments later Trent walked back into the diner and headed straight to the restroom without acknowledging the family as he hurried by. Lou left the table and followed, but Trent had locked himself in one of the stalls, demanding that Lou go back to the booth.

"But..."

"For God's sake, give me some space!"

Lou returned to the family. No one commented on Trent's absence. Lou picked up a few color crayons and joined the children coloring in color books the waitress had brought to the table. The silence became too noisy for Dolores, so after a while, she asked if Trent was sick and wondered if someone should check on him.

"He's having a rough time," Lou explained. "After a long illness, his wife passed away only three months ago. She was just 53 years old. I can't begin to tell you how terrible her death was, and his daughter is missing."

"You don't have to explain anything to us," Dolores interrupted.

"He blames himself for his daughter's disappearance. They had a terrible argument before she took off. Trent was just talking with a private investigator he hired to find her. He calls every day to give Trent a report. Every day, the news is heartbreaking..."

"The poor man," Dolores whispered.

"Hey, everybody, I'm sorry it took me so long to get back to you folks," Trent said while shoe-horning himself back in the booth. "Where are my crayons, kids?"

"You can use mine," Briana said, handing over a yellow crayon.

Everyone at the table noticed Trent's red puffy eyes. Lou hadn't seen him shed a tear since Alexandra's funeral.

"Who would like to have a chocolate sundae...raise your hands," Trent blurted out, smiling. The children raised their hands almost quicker than he got the question out.

"Now, children, you've already had enough to eat, don't you think?" Dolores said grinning at Trent. "You don't want to get a tummy ache, do you?" The waitress brought a sundae for the children to share. The adults couldn't take their eyes off the happy kids devouring the mound of vanilla ice cream, chocolate syrup and whipped cream with nuts sprinkled on top.

"Lou, I have an idea. After we pay the bill, drop me off at home, and you can take David and the family shopping. Dolores can pick out whatever they need. Money is no object, so just have a good time."

"But," Dolores broke in, "you've already done too..."

"No buts about it."

"It sounds great to me," Lou said, winking at the kids who were giggling with excitement and a sugar-high.

The drive to Trent's home was quite the eye-opener for the family. The palatial Victorian estates in the neighborhood must have looked like a magic kingdom. Everyone was invited in for cookies and milk, but no one had the stomach to eat a thing. Dolores spent some time alone, looking at Trent's family photographs lined up on the ornate mantel in his living room. She felt like an intruder in a deceased woman's home.

CHAPTER ELEVEN

After Lou and the family left, Trent stayed home to make a few phone calls. Later on he backed his black 1939 Packard out of the garage and headed toward the Sunset District. He pulled up in front of a house-for-sale on 12th Avenue. Bryan Jeffreys, a real estate agent friend, was standing on the curb waiting for him to arrive. They toured the empty three bedroom two bath house. For a multitude of reasons the house fit perfectly with plans Trent was formulating in his mind for David's family.

After signing papers to purchase the house, he called Bob Davis, the owner of a large furniture outlet in the city. He described the needs for each room, leaving it up to Davis to fill the order from his inventory. Trent had worked with him in the past, and had complete confidence he would get the job done right.

Trent remained in the empty living room for a while, figuring that if Dolores decided not to live in the new house, he could use it as a rental. Staring through the large bay window that faced the upper middle-class neighborhood, he felt a sense of satisfaction he hadn't experienced for many years. He locked up the house and walked down the street to a convenience store to get a snack. Sitting on a bench with his bag of pretzels and a can of Coke, he called Lou to give him the address.

A Catholic church was right across the street from the house. It looked like a small version of some of the cathedrals Alex and Sophia loved visiting when they traveled through Europe. Trent hadn't been in a church for many years, not until Alexandra's funeral. He never appreciated the ways of religion. He considered men who frequented churches weak. During the final years of Alex's illness, Trent sometimes wished he could have had the faith his wife embodied. She was the opposite of the religious hypocrites he had dealt with in business and city government. Through the years he had played hardball with the worst of them.

Trent felt compelled to go inside the church. When he opened the ornately carved oak front doors, smells of incense hit him right away, flooding him with memories from childhood. There were only a few people sitting inside the church, and he didn't want the echoing of his footsteps to disrupt the mostly elderly women, so he sat in a back pew. Not thinking. Not praying. Just being. He didn't realize an hour had gone by when he walked back outside into the bright sunshine.

Lou was pulling into the driveway of the new house just as Trent was leaving the church. The family's arrival turned chaotic. Trent had to put a stop to all the yelling, clapping and hugging going on. Everyone pitched in, carrying bags of clothes, linens, toiletries and 12 bags of groceries.

Dolores was overwhelmed by and very grateful for the new house. She sobbed in Trent's arms.

She shook new bed sheets onto the living room floor and everyone sat down to eat dinner that night. After a prayer of thanksgiving, she delighted in serving everyone a scrumptious feast of hot dogs, pork and beans and canned corn. The paper plates they ate on looked like fine china to her, and she said so. After dinner, the children had just fallen asleep on the floor when the doorbell rang a few times, followed by impatient pounding.

"All right, hold your horses," Trent shushed through the door. He let the delivery men in, and they proceeded to carry in the truckload of furniture. Trent told them where to put everything while Lou and David helped Dolores make the beds and fill the dressers and closets with new wardrobes and linens. By midnight, most everything was in order and the children were asleep in their new beds.

"Don't you need to be back in class tomorrow, I mean this morning?" Lou asked.

"Oh my God, I forgot what day it is. I have to get going!" David gasped.

"I'll drive you, don't worry."

"You've done enough, Lou. I'll call a cab to take him down to Stanford," Trent said picking up the phone.

David wiped tears from his eyes while hugging his mother good-bye. After thanking the men, he got into a waiting cab.

It was 1 a.m. by the time the men left. Dolores locked the front door of her new home. She slumped to the floor and bawled like a baby.

CHAPTER TWELVE

Trent and Lou pulled up to Dolores's house late the next morning. It was recess at the Catholic grammar school across the street. The noise of children playing enticed Trent to take a closer look.

"Come on, Lou, let's go watch the kids, it sounds like they're having a great time."

"Nah, I want to see if Dolores needs help around the house. Maybe I'll take Briana and Matthew for a walk or play games with them."

Trent stood outside of the school yard with his fingers laced through the diamond-shapes of the tall cyclone fence. He found himself mesmerized as the uniform-clad kids swung from a jungle gym, chased each other around the schoolyard and played Dodge Ball which had been his favorite game when he was a kid.

"Excuse me, sir. Do you have a child in our school?" Trent hadn't noticed the nun approaching. "No, Sister, I...I was just wondering if I could meet with the principal sometime today. I have two children I would like to talk to her about."

"I am Sister Denise, and as soon as recess is over I'll be happy to meet you in my office, Mister?"

"Oh, I didn't know you are the principal…my name is Trent Martin. Thank you, Sister." He was surprised that he felt as nervous talking with a nun as he did when he was a boy. The nun smiled as she turned around and quickly headed back toward some children playing in the center of the schoolyard. Her white veil blew up behind her as she walked into the wind. The nuns had been kind to Trent when he was a boy. She looked like one of his favorites.

"Dolores," Lou called from the laundry room where he was going through the last of the belongings she carried on the streets. He was sitting Indian-style on the linoleum floor next to the washing machine reading something on a wrinkled piece of binder paper he had found in an old paper bag. Dolores walked in, and as soon as she saw what he had in his hand, she rushed in and attempted to snatch it away from him. He put it behind his back and stood up. "What is this, Dolores?" he questioned, holding the paper high over his head.

"Give it back to me, that's mine," she yelled while trying to reach it. "Give it back to me, its garbage, throw it away!" she begged with veins bulging on her neck. Dolores left the laundry room and went out the front door, slamming it behind her. Lou couldn't figure out what had just happened. He went after her and found her sitting at the top of the front stairs, crying. The children were watching cartoons, so he partially closed the front door and sat down next to her.

"Would you please tell me what this is? Your name is signed on the bottom…did you write this?" he asked, putting his arm around her shoulder.

"Yes, I did, I thought I threw it away, it's not yours," she whimpered.

"I'll give it back to you if you want, but I have to tell you that this is the most beautiful yet heart-wrenching poem I have ever read. I don't understand."

"I will tell you about it, but it's difficult for me." She wiped her eyes dry with the hem of her apron. "You'll notice that David's name and school are printed on the top of the page," she said, pointing to the left corner. "He would have been contacted by whoever found our bodies. I truly thought that we were going to die out there. This was to be my last will and testament, for God's sake. My children must never see it. I had nothing else to leave behind."

"Dolores, may I please keep it? I promise, no one will ever see it."

"You can have it. I don't ever want to see it again, but you must never show it to anyone," she warned, staring Lou straight in the eye. She got up and straightened out her apron, and looking down at him, she said that he could call her Mama if he'd like to. Lou thanked her, while shoving the poem into his jeans pocket, patting it once.

———

Sister Denise sat at her desk with her hands folded as if she had all the time in the world. "Thank you for waiting, now how can I help you, Mister Martin?"

"Thank you for meeting with me, Sister. I hope you can help me, I have a problem."

Trent told her about Dolores and her children's horrible ordeal while living on the streets and about finding them. The nun teared-up while she listened to the story. He asked if Briana and Matthew could be enrolled in the school and if Dolores could do volunteer work to help in any way. By the time the two hour meeting was over, the children were enrolled in preschool and Dolores had a paying part-time job in the school library. Before leaving, Trent wrote a generous check to the school, along with tuition paid in full through eighth grade.

Trent had never been hugged by a nun before.

Dolores sat stunned while Trent told her everything he had arranged right across the street for her at the school. The house was paid for and he promised that she would receive a monthly check to help take care of her and her family. He told her that if the arrangements weren't what she wanted, that he would change everything to her liking. She thanked him for everything, finding it difficult to talk through the tears.

The children were taking naps when Trent and Lou hugged Dolores good-bye.

———◆———

Alone in his room that night, Lou re-read Dolores's poem. He wept.

In case of emergency contact:
David James
Stanford University

Blessed are the poor who rise up every morning,
No matter the conditions, sunny or wet storming.

The pains of life are too much for stomachs that
are hungering,
The price we'd pay for giving up is starve and go
down blundering.

I want to tear this paper house and rip it all
asunder,
But I dare not move I mustn't move, my children
will uncover.

Their tiny bodies are asleep and are forgetful now,
When they wake up they'll beg for food, again I'll
sob but how?

I'm looking at their matted hair, the heads I

pushed to life,
Tears roll down my sunken cheeks' cause now
they're full of lice.

I mustn't move I will not move, would wake them
from their rest,
They might be dreaming of the days when we were
living best.

It wasn't very long ago when we were family four,
Then daddy took his bottle and abandoned out our
door.

We nar ate much but mush and such, but water
was a plenty,
Now I'd give my life to see my children lick plates
empty.

I am too weak to search for work, plus who
would watch my children?
I'm hungry, tired and dirty, and my wardrobe isn't
willing.

The shelters for the poor looked fine, but they
were very scary,
No telling which crazed drunken man might kill us
but not bury.

It's best to starve and die out here on pavement's
cold hard land,
Because my babes are safe covered under Mama's
hands.

This dawn my heart beats with a joy because their
coughs have ceased,
Oh my God, they wake up not ... have you their
souls released?

I shake my babes with all my strength, son and
daughter do not move.

My heart is breaking, I been faking, been three days since they been waken.
Oh my God I'll hug them tight, please take me from this crushing plight!

Do I hear, oh do I hear wings around me fluttering?
"Come up come Mama, please come home," my soul hears whispers uttering.

I'm rising up I'm flying up and when I look back down,
Three bodies are seen hugging close there on the freezing ground.

Our cardboard house is torn apart, papers fly through screams of thunder,
Angered angels have been sent by God to rip up mankind's blunder.

The food on Heaven's table fills us up and to the most,
It's God himself who waits on us, he is our heavenly host.

No more hunger, tears, or filth's infested heads,
My children's cheeks are rosy and sleep on soft-cloud beds.

I'm laughing and I'm singing, in white robes we have been clad,
My children are now happy with their Mama and real Dad.

Ms. Dolores James

———◦———

At 10 o'clock in the morning, one month after helping Dolores's family, Trent made a phone call to finalize arrangements for a fundraiser to be held at the Fairmont

48

Hotel. He cradled the phone in his neck while sipping his fourth cup of coffee, and listened to the Food and Beverage Director go over the details.

"Everything sounds perfect, Dieter. Pull out all the stops. This fundraiser will dwarf anything else we have hosted before. Another thing," he continued, "I want a stage set up in back of the head table. It will have to be the biggest you can get your hands on because there will be at least one hundred singers in the choir. I'll need your staff to send out the invitations. Great, Lou will bring the list over tomorrow. Two-thousand a plate will be perfect. Three months will be here before we know it. I appreciate all your help, you've never let me down. Call if any questions arise. It is always a pleasure doing business with you. You too. Bye."

Trent remained seated in his recliner after hanging up the phone. He finished his cup of coffee and read Dolores's poem for the third time. Although Lou had eventually received permission from Dolores to share the poem with Trent, he wished he hadn't, due to the distress Trent exhibited while reading it.

"I'm going to the store, do you want me to pick up anything for you while I'm at it?"

"No thanks, Lou."

Trent jolted when the phone rang. "What are doing down in Culver City? I've been reading about gang-wars going on there. Okay, I'll be talking to you tomorrow."

He gripped the arms of his chair after hanging up. The stress of everything felt like a Sumo wrestler was squeezing his head and chest, causing his body to go numb. He forced himself to take slow deep breaths until he loosened up a bit.

CHAPTER THIRTEEN

The highly anticipated gala was held on October 21st. San Francisco was cloaked in fog. Guests started to arrive at 6:30 p.m. No matter how frequently people attended functions at the Fairmont, electricity always permeated the atmosphere. The opening of the hotel in 1906 was disrupted by the infamous earthquake. Her doors were reopened in 1907, the first of the 'Grand Dames' to rise from the ashes in the city of Saint Francis.

Sparkling like thousands of brilliantly faceted diamonds, massive crystal chandeliers hung from tall ornately carved ceilings. The hotel lobby had white and gold marble floors with purple and gold-leafed velvet dressing the ceiling-high windows like kingly robes.

The black-tie event was being held in the Grand Ballroom to raise funds to build shelters for homeless mothers and their children. City officials from San Francisco and Oakland, Hollywood celebrities and clergymen were seated at the two head tables. The Episcopal bishop from Grace Cathedral went on the stage to begin the night's festivities by saying grace. A 12-piece orchestra played soft background music while waiters wearing white tuxedos began the food service. They moved through the ballroom with such poise they appeared to glide through the tables like ballerinas holding trays of delectable foods high above their heads. The service was so beautifully choreographed it looked like a Broadway production.

The guests were eating dessert when Trent walked up to the podium centered on the stage. As soon as he took the microphone in his hand, everyone in the room rose to their feet in a standing ovation.

"Thank you, thank you," Trent shouted over the din, while dabbing tears. "Please, sit down," he kept motioning with his hands.

"Thank you, thank you again." Most of the attendees hadn't seen Trent since Alexandra's funeral almost a year before. It was obvious that most had paid big bucks just to catch a glimpse of Trent Martin again. He hoped that the evening would be the highlight of his life. Actually, it wasn't about him at all.

"Thank you all for coming tonight. We must dig deep to reach high. We *are* our brothers' keepers. I don't want to sound like a preacher tonight, but you know what I have come to realize? To be fully human, we must be willing to serve those less privileged than we are. For the first time in twenty-seven years, I stand here without Alexandra by my side. But I know she is here in spirit, cheering us on in this endeavor."

The crowd rose to its feet again. The applause and whistles were deafening, the room buzzed with love for Trent and his deceased wife.

"Thank you so much. We will have a twenty-minute intermission now, and then we'll continue with tonight's program."

Lights dimmed on and off, announcing the end of the intermission. The guests returned to their tables.

"Looking around this room tonight, I see the faces of friends and colleagues I have known and worked with for years. You are all heroes in my book. You have given of your time, talents and financial support to causes you have adopted such as The American Cancer Society, the Leukemia Society and recently, the Foundation for Aids Research. Everybody, give yourselves a big hand!" Trent shouted, while applauding the 950 guests. The room erupted with explosive applause and whistles. Trent could always stir a crowd up; this night was no exception. It took a few minutes for everyone to be seated again. A hush came over the room.

"I especially want to thank you for responding so positively to the invitation for tonight's event. As you well know, the reason for this fundraiser wasn't given on the invitations. Each of you coming tonight for an undisclosed cause touches my heart deeply. I have a story I want to share, but instead of listening to me go on and on, I invite you to sit back and watch a documentary we put together. Thank you."

A wall-sized screen descended from the ceiling to the floor. The lights dimmed and the film began. The 40-minute documentary transported the audience into the lives of homeless mothers and their children, living next to and under the hustle and bustle of two of the most affluent metropolitan cities in the country. The film crew Trent hired to produce the black and white documentary did a superb job of interviewing and filming homeless mothers and their children living on the streets of San Francisco and Oakland. With the women's permission, the crew filmed the lives of three homeless families for a 48-hour period. Nothing was left to the imagination. Nothing. Each story differed, but all revealed a steadfast resolve to survive while trying to protect their children from elements that daily threatened to harm them. The film was riveting. Guests throughout the ballroom could be heard sniffling.

Just as the atmosphere reached a morose tenor, the film changed from black and white to Technicolor. Across the middle of the screen came the words:

NO MORE!

The film moved from city alleys and streets, to showing Trent interviewing Willy Da Rosa, the President and CEO of Cantilever Construction, one of the Bay Area's most prestigious construction companies. Da Rosa was shown presenting Trent with a slide show detailing the architectural plans and cost projections for two residences for homeless mothers and children in both cities. They would be drug and alcohol-free facilities, with nurses on duty 24 hours a day. A chapel would be built in the center of each home where Sunday services would take place. The doors would always be open for private meditation that could heal hearts and inspire dreams not yet realized. Graduation would take place each year to mark the time when families would be expected to go out on their own with support from entrepreneurial corporations in the community. Once they had become contributing members of society, the graduates and their children would be encouraged to return as volunteers, to mentor new and arriving residents.

The grand finale showed huge water-color paintings of the two homes surrounded by pristine landscaping, concluding with the name of the residences:

~ Mama's Arms ~

When the lights went back on, Trent and Lou were standing up at the podium.

"Well, my friends, I am sure I don't need to introduce you to Lou, the backbone of the Martin family, forever, it seems. To tell you the truth," he joked, "Alexandra said many times that he would have made a better husband than me." The crowd burst into laughter, as Lou took a bow, grinning.

"Don't you go anywhere, Lou, because without your help, tonight wouldn't have been possible. Without any further ado, I want to introduce you all to a wonderful young man. Come on up here," he waved to David standing off to the side of the stage. "This is David James," Trent said, shaking his hand. "He will graduate from Stanford University next spring with a 4.0 GPA, he plays power forward on the Cardinal basketball team and has a heart bigger than all outdoors." The men hugged. He handed David the microphone. David told the crowd about how they all met on the plane returning from Maui. He explained how the encounter led to rescuing his mother, little sister and brother from living on the streets nine months earlier. David spoke with intelligence and sincere humility, captivating every heart in the room. When he finished speaking, the hundred member choir filed onto the stage, forming lines in back of the men. They stood motionless in their long red satin robes, as David handed the microphone back to Trent.

"I would like to introduce you to the woman who inspired the vision for the future *Mama's Arms*. David, would you please bring our Guest of Honor onstage now?"

The audience watched as David walked off the stage, and returned with his mother on his arm. Dolores wore a floor-length royal blue sequined gown, looking years younger than she had only months before. "Everyone," Trent said, putting his arm around Dolores's shoulder, "I would like to introduce you all to David's mother, Miss Dolores James. She has kindly agreed to read you something she wrote." A hush came over the room.

Dolores took the microphone, and began speaking with the confidence and poise of an experienced orator. "Thank you, Mister Martin and Mister Vindigni. Thank you, my son. Thank you all for coming tonight. I especially thank God for sending these angels to save my family. I will read you something I wrote when I was living on the streets, when I thought there was no hope, no tomorrows. Please listen to it as a voice for all the homeless mothers and children who are still cold and hungry tonight, somewhere on our streets. Thank you for helping countless families you'll be helping with your generosity. God bless you all."

Dolores read her poem. Tears fell not only from her eyes, but were seen throughout the room. When she finished, no one knew how to respond to what they had just heard. After a moment of silence, one man stood up and began to applaud, then another, then another, until the whole room rose in a standing ovation, shaking the chandeliers like an earthquake.

Trent went down the stairs and returned, holding the hands of Matthew and Briana. The little guy was dressed in a white tuxedo, and Briana wore a floor-length powder blue velveteen dress. The sight of everyone hugging on the stage resembled a Norman Rockwell painting.

The choir began singing, "There's a Place For Us", from the movie, "West Side Story". Everyone rose to their feet while listening to the hope of *Mama's Arms* embodied in the prophetic lyrics.

Trent thought he could feel Alexandra's arm around his shoulder.

CHAPTER FOURTEEN

While sitting in the dining room eating breakfast, Trent and Lou robotically exchanged sections of the SF Chronicle. The phone rang.

"Hey Vern, how are you? Yes, he's here. Bye." Lou gave the phone to Trent, and sat down to drink another cup of coffee.

"Good morning, how're you doing? Yes ... are you ... all the hospitals?" Trent's jaws clenched while he listened to Vern's report. "Spare no expense ... I know. Thanks for calling. I just thought that Sophia ... talk to you tomorrow." He hung up and slumped in his chair, looking older than he had five minutes earlier. He pressed the palms of his hands against his temples.

"You're getting another one of those headaches. Maybe you ought to have Vern call every other day, this can't be good for your health, Boss."

Trent looked ready to explode.

"She's never coming home and it's all my fault, Lou. Damn it to hell!" Tears welled up in his eyes.

"It is *not* your fault."

Maybe I traveled too much, trying to make more money, but it was for my family. I adore Sophia, but she obviously doesn't know it or she'd be home by now. It's been over two years, Lou."

"But ..."

"Don't interrupt me. Just listen for a change. Sophia was so close to her mom and me, and then Alex began disappearing into Alzheimer's!" he shouted. "Drugs and seedy men became her daddy. I just want another chance to do it right. I need my little girl."

Trent wiped his eyes and took a deep breath, regaining some composure.

"You are the best friend I've ever had, I really don't mean to take everything out on you. I don't know what's wrong with me."

"Forget about it, Boss, I can't begin to understand what you're going through."

"I have a question for you. Do you still think Vern is the right man for the job?"

"I'll put it to you this way, I worked with the guy for ten years and his reputation can't be beat. Believe me, Vernon Rush puts the FBI and CIA to shame. He's the kind of guy who'll frisk a gorilla to find a flea. If she's out there, he'll find her."

"Do you ever miss being a P.I.?"

"Not really. First of all, I was never all that good at it. But that's also about the time my gambling addiction took over. I must have thrown every cent I earned at the craps tables back then. Well, I better get back to my cleaning."

Trent got up and walked to the living room. The mantel above the fireplace was like an altar where everyone he had lost was adored. He was consistently drawn to Sophia's First Communion picture, showing him and Alexandra hugging their little angel. "Bella" is what they called her, meaning beautiful. Trent began to feel light-headed, which often happened when emotionally over-loading on family photos.

He went upstairs where Lou was vacuuming.

"I'm in the mood to go to the airport today. I need to be around people who are on the move. In fact, pack us some clothes just in case."

Trent felt a surge of energy coursing through him as he showered and shaved.

"Damn it, we could go to a movie, a park... anywhere but to the airport. Whatever. I know that once he sets his mind on something, it's over," Lou grumbled to himself, while stuffing clothes and toiletries into two carry-on bags, just in case.

CHAPTER FIFTEEN

Trent took a seat near Gate 16 in the American Airlines terminal. He was reading Sports Illustrated while Lou spent his time in a bar close-by. Lou never missed a Giants game and today was no exception. It was the top of the 7th inning, the San Francisco fans were going wild because the Giants were beating the LA Dodgers 4-2.

Trent's attention was drawn to loud commotion going on at Gate 18. He got up, left the rolled up magazine on his seat and walked toward what was escalating into an alarming disturbance. He expected to see airport security run past him to put a stop to the obnoxious man's outburst. He leaned against a wall facing the commotion, positioning himself strategically to get a clear look at what was going on.

A well-dressed elderly man, who had pushed his way behind the ticket agent's counter, was shouting obscenities in her face. The old guy was bald, short and stocky, and his raging was visibly intimidating to everyone crowding around. The flabbergasted young agent appeared close to falling apart when she yelled for a supervisor's help.

"Don't smart-mouth me, lady, I want my money back. Don't make me tell you again!" he continued to yell at the top of his lungs.

"Calm down, sir," a supervisor shouted, folding her arms and repositioning her feet in a wider stance. "You already purchased a round-trip ticket. We cannot, I repeat, we cannot refund the money for the return leg."

"Read my lips," the man continued his tirade. "I am not returning to San Francisco, miss, and I am never flying on your frigging airline again!"

"Excuse me," a male supervisor showed up, motioning the agent to get out of his way. "Step out from behind the counter, now!" Without giving the belligerent man time to respond, the supervisor pressed his body into him, shoving him into a corner further away from the gate.

"Listen to me. You purchased a round-trip ticket to Las Vegas. We don't give refunds but you can use your return miles for another trip. Your flight leaves in half an hour and if I hear one more word out of your mouth, not only will we keep you off the flight, but security will arrest you. Do I make myself clear?"

The old man was ready to fly off the handle again when he noticed a couple of policemen standing close by with their hands clasped behind their backs, just itching to cuff and drag him away. He grabbed his carry-on bag off the floor and walked towards the bar. The police followed him. Trent followed the police.

From the entrance to the bar, Trent caught Lou's eye, motioning him to come out to the lobby. Lou slammed his bottle of beer on the counter and left the bar. It was the top of the 9th inning.

"What do you want … it's the best game of the year!"

"Sorry, but the flight to Vegas will be boarding in a few minutes. Please go to the counter to buy us a couple of one-way tickets … quick. I want to keep an eye on a guy."

"You are losing your mind!" Lou shouted over his

shoulder as he headed toward the ticket counter.

Trent and Lou were the last to board the flight.

"So we are following someone to Vegas, someone you don't know, for no rational reason," Lou whispered through clenched teeth.

"Just listen. See that bald guy up there? Keep your eye on him. I don't want to lose him at the Vegas airport either. I want to see what he's up to, there's something about the man that scares me. I feel like I could end up like him, the pathetic human being."

"I'm the one who's going mad. Actually I'm pissed, so leave me alone. You made me miss the end of the game for what? So we can follow some whack job," Lou snapped, jerking his seatbelt hard into the fastener.

"I don't want to talk anymore, Boss, just wake me up when we land."

The flight was uneventful. Lou slept for most of the flight. Trent's attention was fixed on the top of the man's head, as if he might disappear from the plane at 35,000 feet.

"Hey," Trent whispered, poking Lou with his elbow, "look at the little girl to our left. She looks like my Sophia … for a second I thought she…doesn't she look like her?"

"Yea, she does, when she was about six years old. But Sophia was prettier," he said, patting Trent on the shoulder in an effort to settle him down.

Trent's heart pounded and his forehead dripped with sweat whenever he was hit with apparitions of his daughter. They came more frequently as the months went by. Sometimes he saw his daughter grown, sometimes a youngster.

CHAPTER SIXTEEN

It was 9 p.m. when the plane landed at McCarran International Airport in Las Vegas. Trent and Lou lined up in back of other passengers gathering their carry-on luggage from the overhead compartments. Parents with crying babies, restless toddlers, and all manner of confusion was going on while everyone vied for a quick exit. Trent's anxiety rose while he struggled to keep an eye on the old guy, while the passengers edged closer to the exit. Trent took off, zig-zagging up the line, apologizing as he pushed his way through passengers in front of him. The old man got out of sight. Lou was stuck in passenger-gridlock about 10 rows behind Trent.

Trent reached the exit and rushed into the terminal, catching sight of the man walking through the outside doors and getting into a cab. Trent flagged down the next available taxi and got in the back seat. Lou made it just in time to jump in while the door was still open. The forward-motion while screeching away from the curb forced the door to slam shut, almost clipping Lou's foot. Trent leaned between the two front seats yelling commands at the cabbie.

"Just follow that cab, we can't lose him. I'm glad you finally decided to show up, Lou … stay on his tail."

"Next time, that is if I continue working for you," Lou quipped, "I won't go anywhere halfcocked with you again. You were going to leave me behind. You've lost your marbles!"

The driver weaved in and out of traffic trying his best to keep up. Horns blaring, oncoming headlights and tail lights on the cars in front of them made it difficult to keep track, especially when they arrived on the Strip. Without warning, the old guy's cab made an abrupt U-turn at a yellow traffic light. Trent's cabbie cussed as he slammed on his brakes when the light turned red.

Without warning, Trent's driver pulled into the circular driveway of a small hotel and jerked to a stop.

"What the hell are you doing?" Trent yelled, glaring at him through the rear view mirror. The cabbie opened his door and slammed it before pulling Trent's door open with such ferocity that the hinges slammed the door shut again.

The enraged driver yelled, "Get the fuck out of my cab!"

Trent jumped out and got right up in his face. "What the hell is going on, you idiot? I told you not to lose that cab!"

"What do you want me to do? We lost the cab, it's gone, alright asshole? It's not my problem if you don't know where the hell you're going." He then turned and yelled at Lou, "Get out!"

Realizing he was in the wrong, Trent backed away from the fuming cabbie.

"I'm sorry. I really am," Trent said, lifting the palms of his hands up, as if surrendering. "Please, just drop us off at Caesar's Palace."

Without saying a word, the driver sat down and started

the engine. Trent and Lou jumped back in, relieved that cooler heads had prevailed.

He dropped them off at the entrance to the hotel and tossed them their overnight bags. As soon as Trent handed the cabbie a wad of cash, he slammed the door and burned rubber on his way back up the Strip, while Trent and Lou were left standing in the exhaust.

———◆———

"I need a drink," Trent exhaled, as they walked into the lobby of Caesar's Palace. Lou went to the front desk to find out where the nearest bar was. They sat down and Trent ordered a bottle of Screaming Eagle and a platter of hors d'oeuvres.

"I know what you're thinking. We lost the guy and none of this makes sense. Okay, now you don't have to say it, I know this trip is already a screw-up."

"Well, here's to you," Lou said, toasting Trent with a third glass of the tequila-mix. "Everything happens for a reason. This trip might just turn out to be a very good thing. As long as we're here, I'm going to try my hand at the craps tables. Don't give me that look. At least one of us is going to have fun in sin city."

After Lou finished off the second bottle, the men checked into their suite. Lou began putting toiletries and clothes into the drawers.

"Hey, Boss, do you want to go down to the casino with me?" Receiving no answer, he opened the door to Trent's bedroom and found him sound asleep on top of the bed-spread, flat on his back, still fully dressed. He removed Trent's shoes and covered him with a white down comfort-er he found in one of the closets. He rummaged through Trent's bag and found the photograph he was looking for. He carried it to Trent's room, and placed it on the side table next to the bed. The framed picture was of Sophia in her cap and gown after her high school graduation ceremonies, enveloped in her parents' arms. Kissing the photograph was the last thing Trent did every night before going to sleep.

Lou changed his clothes, turned off the lights and left to go gamble.

At 8 o'clock the next morning Lou slowly opened the door to the suite, and was surprised to find Trent sitting at the dining room table eating breakfast.

"Well, good morning, Mister Vindigni," he remarked not looking up from the newspaper. "I hope you didn't lose too much at the tables. Well, come and join me for breakfast, you must be starving. Sit down before the food gets cold."

Shaking the sports page open, Lou squinted, barely able to focus through his bloodshot eyes. Trent poured him a cup of black coffee.

By 9 a.m. Trent was back walking the Strip, amazed by all the construction since he and Alexandra had vacationed there ten years earlier. After walking in the heat for an hour he sat down to rest, indulging in a double-scoop French Vanilla ice cream cone at one of the casino's cafés. He wasn't thinking about anything in particular when he noticed a pretty little girl, about four years of age, sitting with her parents eating hot dogs and drinking Cokes. The petite child had curly long blond hair, blue eyes, and a sweet giggle that pierced Trent's heart.

"Can't I ever get away from it...no matter where I go I see her," he teared up and rushed outside and bent over trying to catch his breath. Standing in the 115 degree heat, he didn't realize that the ice cream cone was melting down his pant leg, dripping on his shoe. He threw the cone into

a trash can, and without napkins from the café, he wiped his sticky hands on his slacks. Everything around him appeared to darken when a scantily-clothed young woman walked up, shoving pornographic pamphlets at him. For an eerie moment he felt captured in her black eyes, looking like empty caverns to him. She looked to be about Sophia's age. Trent shook his thoughts away, and threw the pornography into the garbage can on top of the melted ice cream cone. He walked back up the Strip.

He left a message on Lou's phone, letting him know that he had made dinner reservations for that night at Spago's in Caesar's.

"The reservation is for eight o'clock. I'll see you there, jacket and tie not optional."

⸻⬦⸻

Trent kept glancing at his watch while he paced back in forth in front of the fine dining room. By 9 o'clock he figured that Lou was a no-show.

"Martin table for two," Trent addressed the hostess.

"Mister Martin, you are over an hour late," the middle-aged hostess responded.

"I apologize, but I *am* still hungry," he smiled in the flirtatious way he was famous for in his young bachelor days.

"Well, if you're *that* hungry, why don't you just follow me," she smiled, blushing. "Do you still want a table for two?"

"Yes, thank you," he said, following her through the bustling restaurant.

Trent ate his meal. Before his after-dinner drink he had the server remove the unused place-setting. On his way out he slipped the hostess a sizable tip.

He returned to his suite, undressed, climbed under the

covers, leaned over to kiss Sophia's picture and turned off the light. He laid on his back with his hands folded behind his head and stared at the kaleidoscope of colors reflecting off the Strip onto the ceiling.

He got up the next morning and opened the door to Lou's room. Lou was sprawled out on top of the bedspread, flat on his stomach, fully dressed but missing a shoe. Trent walked over to the window, closed the drapes, closed the door and got ready to begin another day in Vegas. He felt more determined than ever to find the old guy.

After taking a long walk and eating lunch at one of the casinos' all-you-can-eat buffets, Trent headed back to Caesar's. He planned on taking a nap before resuming the search later in the day. He realized that he most likely was only fooling himself, that he probably couldn't recognize the guy if he was standing right in front of him.

On his way through the lobby, Trent heard a commotion coming from the casino. He recognized the boisterous voice coming from one of the craps tables. Just as he suspected, it was Lou, drunk as a sailor on leave and not at all the man Trent knew. He stood in back of Lou for a few minutes, finally tapping him on the shoulder.

"Come on, let's get out of here. You've had enough," Trent whispered.

He shoved Trent's hand away hard, causing Lou to lose his balance. "The night is young and so are we, right ladies?" Lou slurred, as he kissed one of the inebriated women hanging on him while smacking a second one's backside. "Hey, bring us another round of drinks," he snapped his fingers, rudely summoning a cocktail waitress who was walking by.

"How much have you lost? You said you were done with this crap," Trent shouted in Lou's face.

"You're the one who forced me to come here. Lighten up and have some fun for a change. Leave me alone, asshole. On the other hand, you could have some fun with me and my girls, or don't you know how to party like a real man anymore?"

Trent walked away, and when he was halfway to the escalator, he turned around and saw Lou stumbling in front of an elevator with a playmate under each arm. When the elevator doors opened, Lou and the women went in.

CHAPTER SEVENTEEN

Trent ordered room service the next morning and got ready to head back to the Strip. Before leaving, he called Vern. "I hope I didn't wake you up, I know it's early. I was just thinking that my daughter might have changed her name ... yea ... well ... I was just thinking. I know you're working hard. All right, talk to you tomorrow. Bye."

After hanging up the phone, Trent left the suite not looking to see if Lou was in the other room. He slammed the door on his way out.

The next day Lou tiptoed out of the elevator on the 26th floor. It was 11 a.m., and the housekeeping staff was vacuuming the halls. He put one hand over his ear, trying to drown out the shrieking noise the vacuums made. Without a firm grip on the banister, he would have fallen down. He weaved back and forth on his way to the suite, and it was becoming painfully clear to him why he quit gambling, booze and loose women twenty years before.

"He is one son of a bitch," Lou cussed under his breath. "Where the hell does he get off ordering me around all these years?" he slurred. After a few misses, Lou maneuvered the hotel key into the correct position to unlock the door. He tripped into the room and landed flat on his face, knocking over an enormous artificial flower arrangement onto the white marble entryway. He felt degraded, lying in his own vomit. Rolling himself up to a standing position he tiptoed to Trent's bedroom and opened the door slightly. It was clear that Trent had slept in the bed and had already left. Lou washed his face in the kitchen sink, and boiled water for a cup of instant coffee. His head was pounding and his eyes hurt so he didn't turn on the lights or open the drapes. Dark was the only favor the universe seemed to be showering on him.

While leaning on an elbow sipping the coffee, he noticed a piece of hotel stationary laying in the middle of the table. He flicked the kitchen light on, and squinted to read the note:

Lou,

I called the airlines and made reservations to fly home. The flight leaves at 5 tomorrow night. You are welcome to fly back with me if you're sober. Meet me at the front entrance of Caesars at 2. This trip was a mistake. You were right.

Trent

Lou still had the note in his hand when the phone rang, startling him.

"Hello," he whispered into the receiver. "Hi Vern ... fine ... he isn't here ... is there any ... what the hell? It's as if she jumped off the planet. Thanks. I'll tell him. Bye."

Lou slept the rest of the day.

Trent had taken off early that morning, relieved that the fiasco in Vegas was finally coming to an end. He walked to the far end of the Strip, had a cup of clam chowder and half a tuna sandwich for lunch, and spent the rest of the day people-watching. He returned to Caesar's, and killed time browsing through some of the high-end Forum shops. He kept questioning his motive for getting on the flight to follow the old guy to start with. He thumbed through some men's ties, wondering if that is what it felt like to lose one's mind; the demarcation between himself and others had somehow blurred. Twice that day he was taken aback when spotting young women he could have sworn were Sophia.

He felt clammy so he rushed out to the lobby, grabbed a glass of water from one of the waitresses and downed two aspirin. He decided that only one thing would help him feel himself again, and that one thing would have to be on the rocks.

He entered a crowded lounge off the main lobby and sat up at the bar. It felt good straddling a bar stool the way he had on his 21st birthday. Trent's father, Joseph Martin, had taken him to O'Shea's Bar on 10th and Clement to celebrate his birthday. Joseph had been close friends with Johnny O'Shea, the proprietor of the Irish bar, since its opening in 1949. Trent's father knew everybody who was anybody in the city. The night of his birthday, O'Shea surprised Trent and his dad with a real Irish experience. The bar was decorated with green shamrocks and balloons, dancers from the San Francisco Irish Cultural Center did the jig, accompanied by fiddles and bagpipes. Along with about a hundred friends and bar regulars, a few nuns and priests from the church around the corner dropped by for shots of Irish whiskey. Free corned beef and cabbage was served throughout the night. The bar was packed with mostly Irish folks who lived in the avenues and Italians from North Beach. Trent hadn't thought about that night for a long time. It felt like only yesterday. His father passed away unexpectedly from a stroke when he was sixty years old, five years younger than Trent was now. He missed his father terribly. He felt like death was chasing him.

"What the hell you son of a bitch, you watered down my Vodka!" a man's gravelly-voice yelled at the bartender from the far end of the bar. The hair on Trent's arms stood up. The voice sounded familiar.

Trent slid off his stool. Trying to be inconspicuous, he walked to the end of the bar and leaned against the wall in back of the guy. The old man yanked his baseball cap off and slammed it on the bar, demanding free drinks for everyone, while continuing to rant at the bartender. The old guy's head was bald.

Trent couldn't move a muscle. The only thing he was sure of was he refused to lose the bald guy again. The bartender, looking like a bouncer at a club, ordered the old man to leave.

Trent followed him into the hotel lobby. He finally made his move and tapped the old fellow on his shoulder.

"Excuse me, sir?"

He jerked away from Trent. "What the hell is your problem?"

"I'm sorry. I thought you were someone I used to know."

"That's what they all say," he yelled in Trent's face. "You queers are all the same. Get away!" he shouted, shaking his hands at his sides. "I don't want to catch AIDS!"

"Just take it easy, first of all I'm not gay, and I think you owe me an apology for saying so," Trent retorted.

The man turned and walked away. Trent walked alongside.

"That bartender seemed like a real son of a bitch and I'm sure he did water down your Vodka." Trent kept talking, although he couldn't tell if the old man was paying any attention. "Come on, I'll buy you a drink."

Bells rang and loud screams broke out in the lobby because someone had won a $50,000 jackpot on the Wheel of Fortune. Trent took a deep breath and shouted over the noise. "Well, do you want a drink or not? I'm going to have a nightcap in the lounge!"

The old guy bent his ear forward, making it clear he had a hearing problem.

"I don't like drinking alone, and I'm sick and tired of this Vegas scene," Trent shouted, miming tipping motions with his hand, as if downing shots.

The old man broke into a half-cocked smile, and started walking toward a crowded lounge in the east lobby. Without saying a word, Trent followed him to a table and sat down across from him.

"Get me a Vodka on the rocks," he informed Trent without looking at him. The man took his baseball cap off and hung it on the back of his chair.

Trent ordered himself one as well. When the cocktail waitress delivered the drinks, he ordered a platter of hors d'oeuvres.

"I don't usually drink with strangers," Trent remarked. He had spent so much energy trying to find the old coot, he didn't want to lose him before satisfying his curiosity. Trent reached across the table to shake the man's hand. "I'm Trent Martin. It's good to meet you, Mister?" The guy jerked his hand away. Trent didn't miss a beat. "Now it's your turn, what's your name, may I be so bold to ask?"

"Edwin."

"Is that your first or last name?"

"Enough with the questions already. The name is Edwin Richards."

The men downed a couple of drinks and picked at the d'oeuvres. Trent sat back with his hands folded on his lap. He wanted to learn about Edwin, but remembering that the man was hard of hearing, he leaned across the table.

"I have a twenty-four year old daughter. Do you have a family, Edwin?"

"It's Mister Richards to you, and my private life is none of your business. But as long as you're buying, yes, I do have a family if you want to call them that.

"I live in San Francisco, have all my life," Trent continued. "Where do you live?"

"I used to live in Hillsborough. I moved here a few days ago, but I won't be here for long. I'll do things my way, and now that I think about it, this is none of your damn business. And quit calling me Mister Richards. That was my father's name. Family, huh, I'm never going to see that bunch of freeloaders again. How about getting me another drink," Edwin said, slapping his empty glass down on the table.

Trent ordered a second drink for Edwin. He needed time to digest the disappointment he was feeling after expending so much time and energy searching for the guy.

"Well, for your information," Edwin added while nursing his drink, "I have five kids and too many grandkids and great-grandkids. I don't know how many there are, I've lost track. My family all live in the Bay Area, which is way too close for my liking. About my kids...I still can't believe I sired the five of them. They're not a family tree I thought would spring out of me. I wouldn't bet a wooden nickel on a single one of them," he continued, looking like he had vinegar running through his veins. "The only thing in their favor is that they're made in my image. My three sons wasted years coaching their kids in sports. I warned them, first things first…work then play. One of the idiots sold his house to put his kids through graduate school. Damn fools. It's driven me nuts watching their foolhardy choices, paying no heed to the sound advice I doled out over the years."

"I don't know where my daughter is," Trent interrupted, attempting to stop what felt like raw sewage spilling out of the guy's mouth.

Edwin continued his rant. Trent ordered himself another drink.

"Like I was saying, it has never bothered a single one of them to ask me to help pay for their kids' educations. My two daughters? I stopped paying them any mind after they left top-notch jobs to change diapers and wear aprons. They traded their upward mobile careers to wipe runny noses, flushing the doctorate degrees I paid for down diaper-stained toilets! I am out of here!" Edwin snapped, pushing his chair back.

Trent reached across the table and touched Edwin's wrist. "Sit down, man, where do you think you are going? I can't eat the rest of this food all by myself. Help me finish, it's the least you can do after I paid for everything. It's only 7 o'clock, I could have sworn you had more class than to just get up and leave like that."

"Today is my 80th birthday, can you believe it?" Edwin continued, as he relaxed back in his seat, placing the palms of his hands flat on the table.

"Happy Birthday," Trent said without meaning it. "Are you still married?"

"My wife … oh her … my kids favor her, especially the expression in their eyes. I avoid looking at them because of that. They also inherited her weak character. Yep, I'll never forgive her for that, the way she left without saying a word. Six months after the diagnosis, she died. That's all, she died. She let me down."

Trent couldn't believe what he was hearing, especially the way Edwin was talking about his wife. He strained to catch his breath while a lump swelled in his throat. He took a sip of water, and got a tighter grip on the arms of his chair, determined to finish the encounter. He tried to put Alexandra out of his mind so he could focus on Edwin.

"I could tell she was trying to take us all down with her," he said, with squinty eyes that displayed intense loathing.

Trent began to sweat profusely. The buzzing in his ears caused him to feel dizzy and nauseous while he continued to listen to the man he had searched for, for obviously no good reason. He wiped his forehead with a white linen napkin.

"She was only forty-six years old, but she laid around in that putrid attire day after day. Her yellow jaundiced skin looked like wrinkled mustard-colored pajamas. I told her to put some lipstick on her cracked lips. Everything about her turned my stomach. Selfish is what she was, leaving me with all the work. I had to pay three nannies to corral those kids. It weakens me to this day."

You know what?" Edwin continued, "I have never been one who could sit around with boring folk who don't have the intelligence to understand a thing I am talking about. I like your style, Trent. You show me respect."

Edwin pushed his chair back, and without saying a word, he grabbed his cap and started walking away. After hesitating a few minutes, Trent went to catch up to him.

"Hey, Edwin, how about meeting back here tomorrow for a couple of drinks? Let's say at four o'clock?"

"What the hell, why not, I can afford to waste one

more day. Remember, the drinks are on you, young man," Edwin chided.

"I'm staying on the twenty-sixth floor, what floor are you staying on, Edwin?"

"The twenty-sixth floor, huh? You really are a la-di-da, now aren't you? It's none of your business, but I'm staying on the 5th floor facing a parking lot. But who gives a damn, I'm not here to sightsee."

Trent walked toward the elevator, wondering what had possessed him to invite Edwin to meet with him again the next day. Perhaps Lou was right. Maybe he was losing his mind.

CHAPTER EIGHTEEN

Lou spent the night out again, but he remembered to leave Trent a note about Vern's phone call, saying there were some new leads he was pursuing.

Trent wrote a note to thank Lou for the update and that he had found Edwin, the bald guy from the plane. He also mentioned he was considering firing Vern because he suspected he was just milking him for money. In addition, he was postponing their flight home so he could meet with Edwin once more. Trent felt relieved that Lou and he were communicating again, although it had been three days since they had seen each other.

Trent stayed in bed the next day and ordered a late lunch in his room, but could hardly eat, his stomach was so upset at the prospect of sitting down with the ugly-spirited man again. At 3 o'clock he contemplated cancelling the meeting, but ended up going in spite of himself.

When Trent got to the lounge, Edwin was already shelling peanuts at the same table they sat at the night before. Trent waved a cocktail waitress over and ordered a couple of Vodkas on the rocks, and let go of his anxiety, figuring it could be his last chance to decipher the week's fiasco. He hadn't really taken the time to take a close look at Edwin's appearance the night before and found himself unexpectedly feeling a twinge of sympathy for the old man. He looked unkempt, needing a shave and a haircut, and the crop of nose hairs emerging from his nostrils were offensive to Trent, who was meticulous with his grooming. He tried to dismiss the particulars of their first meeting and took a closer look at Edwin. He got the sense that at one time the eighty year old might have been a rather successful businessman. Edwin didn't look well.

"Here's to you, Happy Birthday," Trent toasted him for the second time in two days. Both men were more relaxed than the night before. "So, why did you come to Vegas instead of spending your birthday with your family?"

"They always threw my birthday bashes. Year after year they gave me thoughtless gifts that I hid in my cellar closet. After I die they can split the winnings," Edwin smirked. "My sons-in-law always got me five-hundred dollar boxes of Cuba's finest cigars and sets of 18k gold cufflinks. They know I smoke a pipe, and I never wore sissy cufflinks. I detest cigar smoke, but they insisted on smoking those disgusting brown paper-wrapped shavings of chew in my presence."

Trent ordered himself another drink, without Edwin acknowledging anything but his own monologue.

"The butler has to air my house out for a couple of days after they leave. I have always been glad that the likes of them only come around on my birthdays. Their mediocrity turns my stomach."

Trent interrupted, asking if Edwin would like to split an order of calamari. Edwin motioned an okay with a flip of his wrist while continuing to talk.

"I stopped counting the number of grandkids and great-grandkids a long time ago. Between you and me,"

Edwin whispered across the table, "I don't know any of their names. They all look the same to me. You know how it is with family, after a while everyone looks blended just like a milkshake. I hate milkshakes, they give me gas. Of course you don't have a clue what I am talking about, do you? You've only had to put up with one kid. Anyway, as I was saying, I never get so much as a glance or a how-do-you-do from most of them. Everyone treats me with less respect than a fly that should be swatted. Just wait until the next generation of brat's needs tuition money. They'll never squeeze another red cent out of me ... over my dead body."

"I have two sisters, Edwin. Do you have any siblings?"

"I had, I mean I have a younger sister. At my last birthday party Karen kissed me on the forehead. That's the way our mother used to take our temperatures, kissing us on our foreheads. She could tell if we were really sick or if we were faking it so we could stay home from school. I told my sister that we should try to get together for a visit. You know how the years just fly by. It would only take twenty minutes for my butler to drive me to her place. We could have a cup of tea together, and I could get back in time for my nap. I do need those beauty sleeps you know."

"Where does she live?"

"She lives in one of those affordable housing dumps on San Bruno's east side. I figure what the hell, her husband must still be in a rest home somewhere. I'll never let anyone put me in one of those hell houses. They strap old men to wheel chairs, tie bibs around their necks to catch drool, and give them pills to keep them quiet. The very thought of being diapered, not me. I'm living my last days with pride. Pride cometh before the fall, must have been written by someone who had no pride at all, is how I see it. I told my kids years ago, that if they ever saw me slipping in any way from my authentic genius, call Kevorkian."

"My sister's husband hasn't recognized anyone in years. He is nothing but a vegetable, a stalk of celery is what he is. I told her years ago, but does anyone listen to me? I told her to put him in one of those state-run facilities. No telling how many of those fancy-shmancy homes for the headless she checked out before choosing the most expensive place money could afford. I told her, when a guy has Alzheimer's he might as well be dead. Family, huh, who gives a shit? Last year my kids forgot my birthday cake. Birthday parties make a mess. Two years ago, there had to be six or seven brats closing in all around me. I should have been allowed to blow the candles out by myself. They were mine, after all. No telling the germs I ingested from the saliva spewing out of their slobbery lips. They all got into the act, helping old great-grandpa blow out the candles. Parents nowadays, they don't discipline their children. That's what leather belts are for."

"That's the final straw, Richards. I am done listening to your crap, so shut the fuck up!" Trent commanded.

"I'm done with all of it too," Edwin continued, oblivious to Trent's comment. "There will be no more listening to my family taking turns giving me toasts. After listening to them go on and on about nothing at all, it would be my turn to give some sound advice to the bunch of them. They all squandered their lives, overdosing on sentimentality."

———

All of a sudden, Edwin became eerily quiet, looking disoriented. "Who are you?" Edwin asked, blankly staring at Trent and their surroundings.

———

"Relax, Edwin. I'm Trent, do you remember me?" He handed him a glass of water to drink. Edwin seemed to snap back to reality as fast as he disconnected.

"Get that glass out of my face, what the hell is the matter with you?" Edwin yelled, spilling the water all over the table. "Of course I know who you are. Don't disrespect me, young man!" he shouted, pointing his finger in Trent's face.

"What the hell do you think you're doing, you miserable excuse for a human being!" Trent shouted, slapping Edwin's hand away. Trent threw his napkin at Edwin, ordering him to clean up the spilled water. "Shut up and listen for a change, old man. Do you want to live anymore? Are you sick? You make me sick."

"No and no!"

"For a guy your age, you have a lot of smartass left in you."

"That's reassuring, thanks for the compliment."

"You answered no to both questions. So you're not sick and you don't want to live, right?"

"Bingo, bright boy. I said I like your style. You can actually understand what I'm talking about."

"I'll tell you exactly how well I understand you, Richards. You are one son of a bitch, and a worthless excuse for a man."

Customers in the lounge were watching Trent yelling at Edwin. Not wanting to be seen as being cruel to the old man, he lowered his voice. Edwin attempted to get out of his chair, but Trent got in his face and ordered, "I'm not finished with you, old man. You're going to listen to me for a change. Edwin turned white, the frailty of his age showing for the first time.

"Do you think our meeting was just another mistake in your good for nothing life? Well, it's not. It sounds like your family has tried to get close to you, and for the life of me I can't understand why. Do they know you're in Vegas?"

"It's none of their damn business. They'll find my will. That's all they care about anyway."

"You're a foolish man. Listen to me. Two years ago my wife passed away after suffering for years with Alzheimer's, and she was no stalk of celery, I'll tell you that!"

Edwin, unmoved by what Trent was saying, pushed his chair back, again attempting to leave.

"Damn it, I've been buying you drinks for two days, the least you could do is listen to me for a couple of minutes. I don't know where my daughter is, and my wife died. I have lost my family and here you are, throwing yours away."

Trent stopped talking, noticing that Edwin was fully focused on picking the cuticles around his nails. "Forget it, I don't even know why I'm wasting my time with you." Leaning forward, Trent pushed himself out of his chair. He didn't look back at Edwin as he walked toward the lobby.

He had a tough time making it back to the suite. When he opened the door, the room started spinning. Spots clustering before his eyes caused everything to go dark before he blacked out. Lou woke up from a nap when he heard the fall. Barely coherent, Trent was struggling to get up from the floor when Lou caught him. Lou walked him to the sofa, and covered him with a blanket.

"What time is it?" Trent asked, still half out of it.

"It's seven o'clock, Boss. Just take a rest." Trent attempted to explain what had transpired with Edwin, but Lou put a stop to it. "Listen, we are going home. This trip has been a screw-up from the minute you saw that guy at the airport. I don't want to hear anything more about the bastard. Nothing. We are flying home tomorrow and I won't take no for an answer."

When Lou left for another night of gambling, Trent was asleep on the sofa.

The sun shone in Trent's eyes when he woke up the next morning. For a moment he forgot where he was. Sitting up on the sofa, he squinted at his watch. It was 9 a.m. Out of nowhere, memories of Edwin's comments over the last couple of nights began to replay in his mind: *"No one will ever squeeze another red cent out of me, over my dead body...I moved here a few days ago, but I won't be around for long...they will find my will, that's all they care about anyway..."*

Trent pushed himself off the sofa, and went to the kitchen to make himself a cup of coffee. He felt like an electrical current was shooting through his body while reviewing the conversations with the old man. He called the front desk asking to be connected to Edwin's room. He was told that there is no listing for an Edwin Richards staying at Caesar's Palace.

He couldn't believe his ears, so he called back, but was given the same information. He noticed a flicker of light coming from under Lou's door. Trent shook Lou, attempting to wake him. Unsuccessful, he put the overhead light on, shocking him out of a booze-induced sleep. Lying there, naked as a Jay Bird, Lou quickly pulled the sheet up to cover himself.

"I swear, any court in the land would find me not guilty for murdering you!" he shouted, rubbing his eyes. "You are driving me crazy..."

"Stop. Hell, put your robe on and come into the kitchen. There's coffee waiting for you. We've got to talk."

Lou walked into the room, wrapped in the hotel's white terrycloth robe, sat down to drink a cup of coffee and started chewing on a four-day-old donut.

"This better be important, I only got an hour's sleep. Where's the Alka-Seltzer?"

"Don't move, I'll get it for you, later. You look terrible, but you've got to focus. I don't have time to explain everything, so please just do what I ask. And don't give me any lip, Lou. All right, the old guy's name is Edwin Richards. I met with him twice. I think he either has or is going to commit suicide."

Lou leaned forward to hear what Trent was leading up to.

"I need you to call the long-distance operator and get the listing for an Edwin Richards in Hillsborough, California. Just get the phone number and stay in the room in case I need you to do more."

"Okay."

"I'm going down to the front desk. I'll call you as soon as I get more information. Thanks."

CHAPTER NINETEEN

Trent took the elevator down to the main lobby. He told the young lady working the front desk that he wanted to speak with the General Manager.

"Maybe I can be of help," she said in a perky high-pitched voice and a wide smile.

Reading her nametag, he said for a second time, "Christina, I need to speak to the General Manager, please."

"I am sorry, but he's not available now, but I can try to get ahold of my department manager, if it is important."

"Okay, Christina, I don't want to sound pushy, but there is an emergency in your hotel, and no one can help me except ... "

"And what did you say your name is, sir?" she said continuing to smile.

"I didn't. It's Trent Martin and I am staying in suite number 2610. Is the G.M. on the property this morning?"

"Yes, he is."

"Get him."

———

Kenneth Gerdeau, the General Manager, invited Trent into his office, closing the door behind them.

"Thanks for meeting with me," Trent said. The G.M. sat down at a red mahogany desk, leaned back in his leather recliner and folded his hands behind his neck.

"Please sit down, Mister?"

"Trent Martin."

Trent sat down on a forest green upholstered chair, moving it closer to the desk.

"There had better be a good reason for this meeting. Christina said this involves an emergency in my hotel?"

"I believe it does. I need your help," Trent began, reaching for a handkerchief in his back pocket to blot the sweat on his forehead.

"Four days ago I met an eighty year old man in one of your bars. We had a couple of drinks ... oh forget it ... I won't bore you with the details. Like I said, this is an emergency. The man is a guest in your hotel and I have a feeling he might commit suicide in his room. Perhaps he already ..."

"What makes you think that, and what business is this to me or to Caesar's Palace? Vegas breeds depression in some people, there's nothing new about that. What do you expect me to do about it?" he raised his voice while getting up from his chair.

"You're right, let me make myself clear. Here's the deal. My gut tells me that Edwin Richards, the man I'm talking about, could be found dead in one of your rooms while we waste time splitting hairs. Damn, there is too much to try to explain. It could already be too late."

"Why are you bothering me with this? Why not go to his room and check on him yourself?"

"I tried," Trent interrupted. "I asked the front desk to connect me to his room, but they said there is no one registered by that name here. Maybe he's registered under a different name. He told me his room is on the 5th floor facing a parking lot. I'll pay for any inconvenience, but we need to search all the rooms on that floor."

"Hold it right there. You must be drunk or high to think we could search guests' rooms," he said, yanking the glasses from the tip of his nose.

Trent stood up and yelled at Gerdeau, ordering him to sit back down. He turned around and saw the threatening expression Trent was shooting at him.

"I don't think it's in your best interest to end this meeting, sir. I have stayed at Caesar's Palace for many years, and I've spent a load of money in your establishment. You don't want news to get out about a suicide taking place in one of your rooms, do you? If someone reported a bomb threat in your hotel, and you did nothing to protect your guests, who do you think would take the fall if lives were lost?"

"Are you threatening me, Mister Martin?" he said, leaning against the door with his arms crossed. "Do I need to call security?"

"Listen, I will have no problem taking legal action if it turns out you could have saved this man's life," Trent said, handing over one of his business cards.

"So, you are Martin of Martin and Hunt Attorneys at Law, huh?"

Without saying another word, Gerdeau picked up the phone and called his secretary.

"Just close the door behind you, Wendy," he said as she walked in, clip board in hand. "We have a problem on our hands, and we need to keep this quiet."

"Of course, Mister Gerdeau," the curvaceous forty-something blond answered, sitting down on a chair.

"Wendy Harrison, meet Mister Trent Martin." Trent could tell from her firm handshake that she was all business, which he admired.

Gerdeau filled Wendy in on the limited information he had about Edwin, along with the physical description Trent had provided, and told her to come back to him with any added information she could find. He excused himself from the room, telling Trent he would return shortly.

Legally, Trent knew he didn't have a leg to stand on. He was aware that guests staying in any hotel could sue if their rooms were searched without their written permission. Such action would be considered breaking and entering in any court. If, however, Edwin was in trouble or worse, the search could prove warranted. He questioned his judgment, thinking that perhaps Edwin, or whoever he was, had been suicidal most of his life and had no intention of killing himself now. On the other hand, Edwin did say that he wasn't planning to leave Las Vegas, and that he didn't want to live anymore.

CHAPTER TWENTY

A tall lanky security guard accompanied Trent and Gerdeau up the elevator to the north end of the 5th floor. The GM explained what to expect when he entered guests' rooms, which couldn't be reached by phone first. Trent had a difficult time hearing what was being said because of the incessant static coming from the security guard's walkie-talkie. First, they would call each room. If there was no answer, Gerdeau would knock on the door. If there was no response, he would cautiously enter each room. Trent wouldn't be allowed to enter the hotel rooms so he would wait in the hall. The north and south sides of the 5th floor faced parking lots. Everything about the search would be a breach of hotel protocol.

Tension mounted when each room searched proved fruitless. Trent's sense of urgency overruled every temptation to call the whole thing off. He felt similar panic when searching for David James's family five years earlier.

The men arrived at the 12th room. They were shocked when an obese, naked man jumped off the bed, and with arms flailing in the air, came running towards them screaming obscenities. After profuse apologies and a rapid exit, the GM closed the door.

While bent over trying to catch his breath, Trent quipped, "Did you see the look on that guy's face?"

"To tell you the truth," the security guard quipped, trying to stifle his laughter, "I didn't notice his face!"

The search continued. Trent felt like he had dug a hole too deep to climb out of. With each failed attempt to find Edwin, Gerdeau's impatience intensified. Just as he was opening the door to the fifteenth room, what sounded like a small bomb exploded at the end of the hall.

A few guests came out of their rooms, to see what the commotion was, as the men ran into room # 502. Get in here quick, call 911!" Gerdeau yelled. "Is this your guy?" Trent pushed Gerdeau out of the way, and crouching at the bathtub, he saw blood pooling around Edwin's head, with the smoking gun still in his twitching hand.

"He has a pulse," Trent yelled, repeating the order to call 911.

"Don't touch him," Gerdeau ordered.

Security guards blocked the front of the room with yellow police tape. The fire department and police arrived within minutes. Ambulance personnel carefully lifted Edwin out of the tub, took his vitals, and carried him out on a gurney. Police took the .38 caliber Smith and Wesson out of Edwin's hand and bagged it. Finger prints were being dusted and swabs taken from every surface in the room. Everyone wore rubber gloves and paper booties over their shoes to prevent contaminating the scene. Trent, exhausted, sat on a chair near the window facing the parking lot Edwin had mentioned. A policewoman had told Trent to stay put.

The 5th floor elevators were blocked from opening onto the floor, while police escorted all hotel guests, staying on that floor, down the stairs to a basement meeting area. Everyone was questioned about what they had seen or heard in or near room 502 that day.

Trent flinched when a plain-clothed detective shocked him out of his stupor. "I need to see some identification," the detective from the Las Vegas Police Department said. "I am Sergeant Jim Cokas," he said, showing his badge.

After Trent showed the officer identification, the detective started asking questions.

"How well do you know the victim?"

"I met him four days ago. I felt sorry for the old guy, and because of the way he was talking, I got the feeling that he intended to do away with himself. My instincts were right. I don't feel like talking anymore, I need to get some fresh air," Trent said, getting up from his chair.

"Please sit back down, this will only take a few more minutes," the detective said while turning a page on his clipboard. "To make it easier, the General Manager already filled me in on most of the story leading up to finding Mister Richards. Do you have any idea who the people are in this photograph we found on the bedside table?"

Trent took the picture frame and studied the black and white photograph.

"Edwin told me he had a wife and five children, so I would imagine this has to be when they were younger. By the way, Sergeant, is Richards his real name?"

"Yes, we checked his driver's license," he answered.

"Just a couple more questions. Did Richards appear to have his wits about him when you last saw him?"

"Yes, he made perfect sense, but he was a bitter man and seemed depressed and angrier than hell. I just hope the poor bastard comes out of this alive."

Trent overheard a uniformed officer giving an update

on Edwin's condition; he was already in surgery at Vencor Hospital, and was in critical but stable condition.

"Well, are you going to tell us the truth about this Richards guy, Martin?" a policeman Trent hadn't noticed before, asked. "Speak up," the cop said a second time, standing tall and big-bellied, and too close to Trent. Trent yawned while the officer tucked his starched blue uniform shirt snugly into his slacks. Shifting his hips, he pulled up his leather belt and gun holster.

It's no wonder they're called pigs, Trent thought.

"You must know something more about what happened in this room. What are you hiding?"

"Don't talk to me like that. I saved the guy's life, or aren't you aware of that?" Not bothering to look the cop in the eye, Trent continued. "I met him a few days ago, we had a few drinks together and we talked family. You know how that goes, or perhaps you don't. Anyway, he seemed depressed and said he didn't want to live any more. The first time I saw him was five days ago at the San Francisco Airport. We were on the same flight to Vegas and checked into the hotel the same night."

"Why didn't you mention that you and Richards had an argument in the lobby bar last night? We have witnesses who saw you, do you deny that?"

"We did have a disagreement. I am a family man, he isn't. He pissed me off, so I left. I don't know what he did after that. It's starting to stink in here, I'm leaving now."

"You're not leaving this room, I have a couple more ques…"

"Am I being detained?" Trent said standing up.

"Well, no, but …"

"Well, then I'm free to go."

Trent calmly walked out of the room. When he got back to his suite he showered and went to bed.

CHAPTER TWENTY-ONE

Trent was still asleep when his cell phone rang at 8 o'clock the next morning. Lou had slept on the sofa all night and was watching the morning news. He rushed into Trent's room to grab the phone before it woke him up, closed the door, and went into his room to take the call.

"Hello? I can't hear you ... Vern? ... it's a bad connection ... okay, that's better. What? Slow down...what the hell? Are they sure? It can't be ... oh my God ... it's going to kill him ... no, I'll tell him. He needs to sleep some more or he'll go mad. I'll call the airlines right now and we'll get there later today. What time does the Medical Examiner's Office close? We'll pick up her dental records on the way. Okay, 4 o'clock. Bye."

Lou made the reservations to fly back to San Francisco early that afternoon.

⸻◦◦⸻

Lou was putting some of his belongings in his duffle bag. Trent walked into the room.

"What are you doing?" Trent asked, not fully awake.

"We need to fly back to the city later today. Our flight leaves at 1:30, so we need to get going. Get yourself a cup of coffee before I explain what's going on."

"Don't play games with me, Lou. Put your things back in the drawer, we're not leaving today. Where's my phone?" he said, unable to find it in his room.

"I got it right here, Boss."

Trent called the hospital, while Lou paced back and forth, waiting for him to get off. He knew Trent was going to fall apart when he told him about Vern's call.

"Good news, Edwin is in Intensive Care and is going to make it."

"I don't want to hear any more about that old man. Like I said before, get a cup of coffee and sit down, we need to talk."

Lou explained that earlier that morning, the San Francisco Medical Examiner had called Vern, informing him that a young woman's partially decomposed body had been found; the remains were a match with Sophia's height, weight, hair color and age, and that the examiner needed them to bring her dental records to him.

Trent showed no emotion. He walked to his room, stiff like a zombie, and packed his clothes.

———

At 1 p.m. the men boarded the flight.

"Two cups of coffee, please," Lou asked the flight attendant.

"Lou," Trent spoke for the first time since hearing the news, "is Vern going to meet us there?"

"No, but he is flying back from Arizona today. Vern had made sure that Sophia remained on the Medical Examiner's radar through the years. He wanted me to tell you how bad he feels, and that he hopes Sophia is still alive and well."

Trent squeezed his eyes closed, as tears streamed down his face for the duration of the flight.

———◆———

"What's the address?" the cab driver asked as they pulled away from the dentist's office.

"850 Bryant Street," Lou answered.

Trent walked into the Medical Examiner's Office alone.

———◆———

The corpse wasn't Sophia.

CHAPTER TWENTY-TWO

During the drive back home, Trent called Vern and fired him. Lou couldn't believe his ears. The first thing Trent did after breakfast the next morning was call the hospital to get an update on Edwin's condition.

Lou was disgusted with the continued preoccupation with the old man.

"The fool is obsessed with other people's lives, and he's wasting mine," Lou muttered to himself before going out the front door. He walked the first few blocks, then began running faster than he had in years. When he got back, he overheard Trent on the phone in the library.

"Hello," Trent was leaving a message on an answering machine, "I am looking for the family of an Edwin Richards. I am a friend of his. I'll call back later. Hey, Lou, is there any coffee left over from breakfast?"

"No!" Lou shouted.

"What's with the attitude?"

"Forget it, Mister Martin. I'm gonna have another shot of bourbon, would you like to join me? Might do you some good."

"What's with the Mister stuff? And with all due respect, I would appreciate it if my driver wouldn't get plastered at eleven in the damn morning. We're not in Vegas anymore, pull it together.

Lou went to the entrance of the library. "Well, with all due respect back at you, I've had it up to here," Lou scoffed, making a slicing motion across his throat.

"What's the matter with you? Yesterday I thought my daughter was found dead, and now you're talking to me this way?"

"I'm sick to death of being dragged around the country by you to get involved with people's lives. I'm no frigging shrink, but not living your own life so you can rescue strangers is nothing but a substitution for failing to help your own daughter."

"Don't *ever* speak to me like that again!"

"I'll talk to you any way I want. You think this is all about you? Yesterday was horrible. I was scared shitless that Sophia was dead, and the very next day you're sitting here making calls about that old man. You've lost your mind, and I'm starting to lose mine. You're not going to pull me around the country like some monkey on a leash anymore. You're a lunatic!"

"Get out of my house!"

Lou took off in the limousine.

Trent leaned back on his recliner, reeling. He heard a man screaming Sophia's name over and over again ... louder and louder. He covered his ears with the palms of his hands, attempting to block out the voice that kept coming at him; like a vacuum sucking him into insanity. He slapped his face when he realized that he was the one doing the screaming.

At 4 o'clock, Trent redialed the phone number. A man answered.

"Hello, I'd like to speak to Edwin Richards."

"He isn't here right now, may I take a message, and who should I say is calling?"

"My name is Trent Martin. I'm a friend of Edwin." The other end of the line remained silent. "Sir, are you there?"

"Yes, I am. I'm Edwin's son, Josh. What is this about?"

"I know where your father is…"

"Elizabeth, come here quick!" Richards could be heard screaming so loud, Trent had to hold the phone away from his ear. "Hurry up, there's a man on the phone who knows where Dad is … hurry up!"

———◆———

The next morning Trent drove down to Hillsborough. When he pulled through the open gate into the property. Edwin's five adult children, their spouses and many children greeted his arrival with controlled excitement. Everyone except the small children watched over by a nanny, sat down at the dining room table. A butler served bakery delicacies, coffee and assorted juices. During his two hour visit, Trent described how he had become acquainted with Edwin, the content of their conversations, disagreement, and the search that led to finding him.

Edwin's sons and daughters described their shock when they realized their father had disappeared without a trace. He had left all his belongings behind, unlike other times when he left on trips. Within a couple of days they contacted the police about his disappearance. The family thought foul-play could be involved, but when the police took down the information, the police surmised it was nothing more than a case of an old man suffering from dementia. They tried to convince the officers that their father was sharp as a tack, but to no avail. Edwin had always been a creature of habit, and the butler testified to that fact when being questioned.

Trent listened while the family described their father as a bitter man since the death of their mother years earlier. They also felt anger towards their dad for the way he treated their mother as she lay dying and the way he spoke of her demise afterwards. But they still loved their father, even though he had never really connected with them unless he was being critical.

———•◦•———

When he got home, Trent was surprised to see his limousine parked in the driveway. He and Lou apologized for their outbursts of the day before. Lou said he would be happy to pack their bags and fly back to Vegas to see how Edwin was doing, if that was what Trent wanted. Instead, the men drank a bourbon and soda together while Trent explained what had transpired with Edwin's family.

"Boss," Lou spoke in a low voice, shaking his head, "I've got to hand it to you, your instincts were right, and you pushed through until you saved the old guy."

Edwin's family flew to Las Vegas the next day. Their cab stopped at a bakery on the way to the hospital, to pick up the birthday cake Trent told them he wanted to donate to the reunion. Within a couple of hours, they stood around Edwin's hospital bed singing *Happy Birthday* to him. They all helped him blow out the candles.

A few months later Trent received a call from Edwin, thanking him for saving his life and giving his family back to him.

CHAPTER TWENTY-THREE

Trent had been suffering with terrible nightmares, which became a nightly occurrence beginning a month after meeting with the Medical Examiner. Lou bugged him for a few weeks before he agreed to see the doctor. Trent's physician, Dr. Grant Galiardi, still made house calls for the close friends. He had taken care of the Martin family for thirty years.

Lou led the doctor to the library.

"Don't bother to get up, you old goat," Galiardi joked, lightly pushing Trent's shoulders back against his recliner. The men shook hands.

"Hey, Lou, would you fix Grant a gin and tonic, that is what you still drink, right? Make yourself at home, it has been way too long."

"Lou, don't bother, but thanks anyway. I still drink now and then, but I'm a bit of a teetotaler now. Oh, what the heck, I could use a drink now. But just remember, Martin, I didn't come here to get plastered like we did in the old days. Where the hell have the years gone?"

"Thanks for the drinks, Lou. To years of friendship," Trent toasted his friend.

"Aren't you going to join us, Lou?"

"Maybe I will next round, Doc."

"Yes," Trent said, reminiscing, "no doubt about it, the sixties were our heyday. How many grandchildren do you and Judy have now?"

"We have six, but that's enough about me. Lou told me you're having a rough time."

"I don't feel like talking about anything, Grant. Lou already told you everything, so let's just leave it alone, alright?"

"It's not alright, just tell me what's been going on."

"My nerves are shot, I can't concentrate on anything, I toss and turn all night, I have nightmares and I've lost my appetite. But other than that I'm doing just fine," Trent said, swirling the ice in his drink around with his finger.

"By the way, is it okay with you if Lou stays here while we talk?"

"It doesn't matter."

Lou sat on a chair in the corner.

"Lou told me about the call you received from the Medical Examiner's Office a couple of months ago. I can't imagine how terrible that had to be. With all you have been through, a weaker man would have totally fallen apart. And on that note, I want you to know how much Judy and I miss Alexandra and Sophia. Our fingers are crossed that Sophia returns to you safe and sound."

"Thanks, me too. I'm sorry, but I just want to be left alone."

"Alright, but will you just listen to what I have to say? I believe you were traumatized just as much as if the girl's remains had been Sophia's. Yesterday I spoke with Walt Orona, the Chief Medical Examiner you met with. He's been a colleague of mine for years. He told me that you showed no emotion when you received the report, and that you left his office without saying so much as a word."

"But it wasn't Sophia, I was so happy it wasn't," Trent spoke slightly above a whisper. "At the same time I feel guilty for being relieved that it wasn't her, and that it meant it was someone else's daughter. I just want to hold my little girl again," his voice cracked as tears flooded his eyes.

"Take some deep breaths," Trent. "Let me try to tell you what I think is going on. That's why I'm here."

"What are you, a shrink now? Do you want me to lay on the sofa, or will the recliner be fine? Give me some pills and we'll call it a day. I'm tired, Grant."

"At least let me tell you what I know so far. Your nightmares began about one month after you saw the Medical Examiner, right? I think you may be suffering from Post-Traumatic Stress Disorder, something a lot of veterans suffer when they return from the front lines."

"Don't compare me to soldiers who have lost their minds..."

"I don't think you've lost your mind, but I do think you need to get it all out, so please just start describing your nightmares."

Trent leaned his head back and closed his eyes.

"It's always the same and it scares the hell out of me."

"Go on, just take your time."

"It's almost impossible to describe. I see an old barn standing in the middle of miles of tall yellow grass ... no, it's more like a skeleton shaped like a barn I guess. Loud winds are howling, making the barn's splintered boards swing, but then they turn into rotted teeth that keep shooting down to the ground. The place is full of rats running around in circles and the wooden darts fly off the barn, aiming for my eyes, trying to blind me! It gets worse," Trent said, glaring into his friend's eyes. "I never want to sleep again, do you hear me?" Trent lost all color from his face like he was going to pass out.

"Here, drink some of this water. You're doing fine, Trent, it's almost over. Start where you are fighting off the wooden darts."

Lou took a swig of whiskey out of a flask and put it back behind his back.

"The rotted barn's fractured roof is turning into a skull growing taller and taller. Its Sophia's face ... she's five years old ... I can't go on," Trent grunted, squeezing the arms of the recliner.

"You really need to get it all out, my friend."

Trent's eyes gaped open. "It's her I tell you. She recognizes me. Oh my God, she's staring at me through the corners of her blue eyes without turning her head. She's screaming daddy, daddy, daddy... she won't stop!" Trent yelled, covering his ears with his hands. "The cobwebs are growing in her mouth, choking her ... she can't breathe. I keep trying to reach her but I'm paralyzed. My little girl ... she's smothering ... vomiting ... I can't save her ..."

Trent exhaled hard. His chin slumped to his chest.

Chapter Twenty-Four

I t was late when the doctor left the house. He gave Trent a prescription for an anti-anxiety/sleeping pill, and also recommended writing in a daily journal. He suggested that Trent write love letters to Sophia, while imagining her reading them someday.

"Well, how are you doing, Lou?" the doctor asked as they walked down the front steps. Lou needed to hold onto the hand rail to balance himself on the descent. He leaned against the doctor's red Oldsmobile parked in front and lit up a cigarette, taking three flicks of his lighter to do the job.

"To be honest, I'm planning to leave this job and find a career where I can call my own shots, if you get my drift," Lou slurred. "Once Trent is on his feet again, I will be out of here so fast all he'll see is my ass and elbows."

"You were always close to Alexandra and Sophia, weren't you?"

"Nice of you to remember, no one else does. Trent thinks he's the only one who lost his family. They were mine too."

The doctor leaned against the car, although the January cold was increasing the discomfort in his arthritic knees and hands. He crossed his arms and ankles, attempting to warm his joints.

"Lou, just tell me what's been going on around here."

"Things really changed after Alex died. I don't understand Trent anymore. He's not the same guy you knew. I'm not going to bore you with all the details, but Trent has morphed into some kind of a do-gooder. That's fine for him, but I don't give a damn about all the people he got us involved with. He has dragged me around to airports where he ended up helping total strangers. Can you imagine that? He's like some kind of a clairvoyant now. I know he isn't crazy or anything," Lou said, throwing his cigarette butt on the sidewalk, grinding it out with the toe of his shoe, "but he's driving me nuts I can tell you that."

"What are you talking about, he helps complete strangers out?"

"Yep. I'll give you an example. It seemed like it started right after Alex died. Trent met a kid on a flight when we were returning from Maui, and he got drawn into helping him out. We rescued his family from a life on the streets. He had hired a P.I. to try and track down Sophia, but he was going crazy, just sitting around the house waiting for phone calls of her whereabouts. Sometimes he wanted to go to the airport every day. He's obsessed. I felt sorry for the guy. Oh, wait until you hear this one," Lou said, lighting up another cigarette.

"Go for it."

"Okay, one morning a few years ago, he informed me that as usual, we were going to spend the day at the airport. That afternoon we were sitting in the terminal when we saw a little girl and her father walking out of a gift shop. They sat on seats close to where we were. The father lifted the little girl onto his lap and they started eating a bag of candy. I didn't see anything wrong, but I'll tell you what happened. She looked like she was having a good time with her dad, but Trent told me later that he didn't feel comfortable with the blank expression on her face, or with the stiff way she held her body. Go figure. It was getting late, so I wanted to head home, but Trent refused to leave when they started to walk away. There was something about the father that grossed him out. You see what I mean, Doc? Whatever. Anyway, we followed them and we sat down within an eyeshot. The man lifted his daughter back on his lap. The little girl was saying 'Daddy,' but the father never said a word. He said he felt a chill shoot through him right then. Trent got out of his seat, saying he'd be right back. He walked past them, turned right around and walked back to me, saying to be ready to follow them if they walked away again. It made no sense to me. He called the Millbrae Police Chief, a personal friend... who doesn't he know personally? Anyway, he made arrangements to have the man followed when they left the airport. Trent told me that if the guy got on a flight, then we would be doing the following. He told the chief maybe he ought to check this guy out because Trent had a gut feeling he was a child molester. Trent always had a way, as you know, where people took his word without good reason."

Lou noticed the doctor was shivering. "That's enough, it looks like you are freezing your ass off. Besides, it's getting late."

"Don't leave me hanging there, so what happened."

"Anyway, when they left the airport, the police followed them home and staked out their house. Would you believe it, just two days later the cops called to tell us that the guy had been running a daycare center as a front for a child sex-ring out of his home."

"Was that the one I read about a few years ago in South San Francisco?"

"Yep, and all because Trent had one of his feelings."

"My God, Lou, I can't get over it. To think that it was Trent who saved all those innocent children ... blows my mind."

"This might sound heartless, but I am so done with all of it, Grant."

"I don't think you're heartless, obviously it's been tough on you. Let me ask you this, after Alex passed away, did Trent ever go back to work?"

"He tried to get back into it, but his heart just wasn't there anymore, so he sold his half of the practice to his partner. He seemed to lose all sense of reality. His friends would call him, but he didn't bother to keep in touch so they stopped. We see his relatives on holidays."

Lou spit on the sidewalk. "It's my life too, you know?" he said before removing a flask out of his jeans pocket, took a swig, and he wiped his mouth with the back of his arm before twisting the lid back on. "I want to move to Vegas. I'll just get a job at one of the casinos or something. I'm finished living Trent's life."

———◆———

Within a couple of months, Trent's appetite had returned and the nightmares had ceased.

CHAPTER TWENTY-FIVE

Things changed radically over the next few months. Once he saw that Trent was back on his feet, Lou finally decided he was done. He left a note saying it was time to start living his own life, and he wouldn't be back.

Trent's mother, Rosa, was admitted to the hospital after a near-fatal heart attack. Near death, the ninety-two year old matriarch of the family was succumbing to heart failure. Trent, his two sisters and their families, adored Mama Rosa. Her imminent passing felt like the heart of the family was being excised. His sisters spent the days with their mother, and Trent remained during the nights. Every muscle in his body ached from the cramped positions he had to take in the fold-up bed the hospital staff set up for him at her bedside. He had a terrible time sleeping, as he struggled with the feelings of failure for the years he wished he had taken more time to spend with his mother. He cupped her hands in his, thanking her over and over again for raising him so well, and for all the ways she encouraged him through even the roughest times in his life. She was mildly sedated so he wasn't sure if she could understand everything he was trying to tell her. He begged her not to die, that he was lonely and needed her now more than ever. He never believed his mother would die, and berated himself for not facing reality. With tears rolling down her cheeks, she tried to comfort her son, petting his head softly.

A royal blue, crystal-beaded rosary weaved through Rosa's fingers. Before slipping into a coma, she told her family that she had prayed the rosary for Sophia's return every day since her disappearance. Her granddaughter had always held a special place in her heart. Being her first grandchild, they had shared many special alone times together. She tried her best to stay close to Sophia during Alexandra's illness, but the drug world had already staked a firm grip on the girl. Rosa told her children that she would not die in peace until she saw her granddaughter again. During the week she remained in the coma, she continued to move the beads, although the rest of her body laid limb. The nurses told the family that what they were seeing was nothing more than involuntary muscle spasms. The family knew better.

Lou's absence from the hospital was noticed by everyone. Trent kept hoping that he would come to visit his mother before it was too late. Some days Trent could tell that Lou had been back in the house by the stink of stale Chanel No. 5 permeating the air. He left a few notes on the dining room table, telling Lou of Rosa's worsening condition. The notes disappeared but Lou never showed up.

Trent's sisters' hearts were breaking as their mother neared death, but their deepest concern was for their seventy year old brother. They were afraid that Rosa's passing would shred him into a million pieces.

⸻⸱⸱⸻

At 6:32 p.m., on April 16th, 2006, Rosa's eyes suddenly opened wide and she pointed to a corner of the ceiling in her hospital room. Everyone in the family saw it. She smiled, looking younger, as all traces of age seemed to disappear from her face. She called out Sophia's name and took her last breath.

Trent was the last one to leave his mother's side. He tenderly unwound the rosary beads from her fingers, and dropped them into his jacket pocket.

———

After the Mass for Rosa, the funeral procession left Saints Peter and Paul Church to drive to the cemetery. Going through the gates of Holy Cross Cemetery catapulted Trent back to his wife's funeral. Riding in the hearse with his sisters, he started to panic. He had suffered such attacks before, but this one really scared him. He gripped the edge of the seat to prevent himself from opening the door and taking off. His heart was pounding so hard he found it difficult to breathe, so he popped a couple of aspirin into his dry mouth, chewing the bitter grains while trying to relax. When the hearse pulled up near the gravesite, he was relieved when he could get out to walk around.

He sat next to his relatives on fold-up chairs in the first row closest to his mother's casket. The priest read some prayers and sprinkled her coffin with holy water. For a brief moment, Trent's attention was drawn across the cemetery grounds, where, about 300 feet away, he could see the figure of a man standing alone. When he looked back a few minutes later, the man was gone. Trent realized it had been Lou.

When the funeral rites were over, everyone was invited to Rosa's house for a reception. Trent was too overwhelmed to visit with anyone, so when the hearse dropped him and his family back at the church, he hugged his sisters, got in his car and drove down to Fisherman's Wharf.

Wandering around aimlessly, Trent reminisced about his life. He recalled how fishermen competed to see who had hauled in the most Dungeness crab. Just like when he was a small boy, he found himself getting caught up in listening to the banter of old fishermen.

During the summer months, Trent worked with his father, who owned a fleet of the fishing boats. From an early age, he worked hard at the most menial jobs. He had inherited his father's natural charisma and work ethic, earning him the respect of family, friends and fishermen.

After buying a cup of cracked crab and a cup of hot black coffee from one of the fishermen standing behind steamy pots, he sat down on a bench in the late afternoon sunshine. He relaxed while enjoying the familiar nourishment and inhaled the fragrance of the salty breeze blowing off the Pacific Ocean. Memories flooded him like a slideshow:

.... He graduated Magna Cum Laude from the University of Notre Dame in Indiana. He earned his law degree from Hastings Law School in San Francisco, and with his father's backing, he and a friend opened the law firm of Martin and Hunt, located in the heart of the Financial District. The Examiner often wrote articles about Trent's part in establishing laws to protect entrepreneurs from monopolistic practices. During his lucrative career, he closely involved himself with City Hall, working to improve race-relations, and invested in financing the building of the Embarcadero Center. Known as one of the city's *who's who*, he was often mentioned in the society pages of the Examiner and Chronicle.

The loud squawking of seagulls circling in formation overhead jerked him back to reality. His father, daughter, and now his mother was gone too. He wasn't the boy with his dad on the pier anymore, and he wasn't the man he had become. Now he was just a lonely old man, a has-been, a nobody. *"Why are you punishing me, God? What have I ever done to you?"*

———◦•◦———

Trent rushed to his car and stomped on the accelerator. Speeding and running through stop signs, he pulled up in front of the church, smashing his fender on the curb. He shoved the doors open hard, rushed up the aisle of the empty edifice and sat down in the front pew. He'd never sat that close to an altar before, and he didn't like it. Bright lights outside, shone through a large stained glass window depicting Michelangelo's *The Creation*. Between the finger-tips of God and Adam touching is where the street lights shot directly onto the bronze body of Jesus hanging on the large crucifix high above the golden tabernacle. Floral arrangements from his mother's funeral that morning remained on stands surrounding the altar. The aroma of death the flowers exhaled stuck to his throat like gravel.

Looking up at the crucifix, he yelled, "Who in the hell do you think you are?" His voice echoed through the house of worship. "You're a liar!" He slid out of the pew and walked up the three steps to the altar.

He pounded the altar with his fists and spit on it, before breaking down laughing, crying. Searing pain burst in his head.

———◦•◦———

Trent opened his eyes, disoriented and unable to move. Slowly, he realized he was flat on his back, staring at the underside of the altar. Lying there, it took a few minutes to recognize that the foot on a step above the rest of his body, was his. The polished black wing-tipped shoe was the dead give-away. His eyes were drawn up to the stained glass window depicting *The Creation*. Everything around him was swimming in circles, he was nauseated.

"Honey, I could live in Rome forever," he heard Alexandra's

114

beautiful voice. *"Look up, Sophia, see God's finger touching Adam's finger? Oh Trent, let's come here every year, it's like Heaven."*

Trent was laughing out loud with his young family again. They were back in the Sistine Chapel in Rome. He delighted in the joy his family shared on their trips abroad.

"Oh, Daddy, it's so very pretty up here," Sophia called to her parents from atop Trent's shoulders. *"Daddy, look, God is so big. I love you, Daddy,"* the four year old kept shouting over and over again.

"Shhhh, Sophia, we're supposed to be quiet here, Honey," he repeated, tickling her.

He was laughing, but he couldn't hear his own voice. The scene he thought real began to fade away, then slowly disappeared. Panic stirred as he struggled to bring his wife and daughter back. His eyes frantically scanned the stained glass window, convinced that Alexandra and Sophia were playing hide and seek behind God and Adam's finger-tips.

"Oh God, forgive me ... I want my family back," he groaned before passing out again.

A priest came walking through the church to lock the doors for the night. The church was dark, but light emanating from the flickering votive candles in front of the church revealed the form of a body lying at the foot of the altar.

"Wake up, sir ... open your eyes ... can you hear me?" the priest called out, shaking Trent's shoulders.

The priest stayed with Trent in the ambulance as he was rushed to San Francisco General Hospital. During the ride, Trent opened his eyes just long enough to catch sight of his Roman collar before passing out again.

CHAPTER TWENTY-SIX

W hile eating lunch in the cafeteria Dr. Abraham said, "I'll tell you this, if I had seen the CT scan before reading the rest of the report, I would have presumed the patient had died."

"No kidding," Dr. Chavez concurred. "The clot was the size of a large egg. I can't imagine he will ever walk again, the poor guy."

"No amount of money can stop bad stuff from happening to anybody, no matter how important they are," Dr. Abraham interjected.

"Why, is this Martin guy loaded?"

"I forgot, you're new in town, but yea, Trent Martin is a pretty big deal. Years ago, you couldn't pick up a newspaper without seeing his name all over it. He's done a lot of good for this city, and to think now he might need to be put in restraints. He keeps trying to pull his I.V. out," he said, getting up from his chair. "I'm going upstairs to do my rounds with Dr. Pompili now. I'll see you back on the floor."

"I'll be up in a few," Dr. Chavez said, not looking up from her coffee cup.

Trent didn't have to be put in restraints after all. His

doctors upped the dose of the medication to keep him sedated. Physical therapists went to Trent's private room four times a day. He was having a tough time trying to learn to swallow. He had suffered a cerebral thrombosis on the left side of his brain, causing right-side paralysis. Therapists exercised his arms and legs frequently, but despite being on blood thinners, there was still a high risk of suffering a second stroke if another clot formed and escaped to his brain or lungs. The array of doctors working on his case depleted the little bit of energy he had.

When Trent struggled to speak, he whispered, "Let me die." His doctors told him he would be moved to a rehabilitation center once he was able to eat baby food. When nurses and doctors tried to talk to him, he closed his eyes, shutting everything and everyone out.

After a month, Trent was evaluated as being ready to go to a rehab center, but he refused. He wanted to go home. The doctors complied with his wishes. A physical therapist was scheduled to continue working with him at his home so he wouldn't backslide from the progress he had made in the hospital. Once a week a psychologist drove to his estate to evaluate his state of mind. He was depressed but returning to the comfort of his own surroundings caused an almost immediate increase in his appetite. Trent rallied, determined to push hard through the daily grind. In a few weeks he was able to sit in a wheel chair to eat his meals.

Trent's sisters visited him regularly, but he refused to talk on the phone when anyone called. He shut most of the world out, telling his family there was nothing left in it for him. After a while, the phone stopped ringing. When someone showed up for a visit, his new housekeeper, Gerda, took care of them in short order. With hands placed on her ample hips, pursed lips and fiery eyes threatening, she successfully scared uninvited guests away.

Sitting on a plastic chair in the shower, a visiting nurse washed his privates, stripping away the last vestiges of Trent's dignity.

———•———

Early one evening, Trent was sitting in his library watching the Giants game. He had just finished his dinner and was moving the tray table aside when he heard someone trying to open the front door with a key. Before he had a chance to call Gerda, the door opened and closed. Within seconds, Lou stood in the doorway of the library, looking down at Trent. The men were speechless. It had been a year since they had seen each other.

"Oh my God, Boss," Lou whispered almost too low to hear, "I am so sorry."

He fell to his knees in front of the wheelchair. He hid his face in his hands.

"Lou, it's not your fault ... strokes happen, what can you do?"

"You don't understand," Lou interrupted. "It's all my fault. I am a fool." Tears streamed from Lou's eyes, landing on Trent's slippers.

"Get a hold of yourself, are you drunk?"

"It's my fault you had the stroke ... that you lost Sophia. I almost killed you, and she might be dead because of me."

Lou was shaking on the floor like a dog in from the rain.

"What's the matter with you, and what the hell are you talking about?" Trent leaned his head back, already feeling drained by the unexpected visit.

"I don't drink or gamble anymore, so get that straight. I came here to tell you the truth." He got up off the floor and sat down on the couch. "When Alexandra's Alzheimer's was getting worse, I couldn't bear to watch her suffering like she was. It was killing me, too. Sophia was only seventeen years old and she was hiding her feelings from you."

"Get to the point, Lou."

"Every night I could hear Sophia crying herself to sleep. Losing her mother like that was tearing her apart. One night, when I figured Alex and you were asleep, I knocked on her bedroom door. When she told me to come in, I took one look at the dark circles under her red eyes, and decided I had a way to help her get some sleep."

"Just spit it out, Lou!" he yelled, leaning forward in his chair. "What the hell did you do to my little girl?"

"Mister Martin, why don't I get you and your guest something to drink," Gerda suggested in her demanding way, nosily poking her head through the door.

"We're fine, Gerda. Just close the doors behind you. Thank you." Trent exhaled.

"Where'd you find the Gestapo?" Lou whispered, hoping she couldn't hear what he was saying.

"Don't change the subject, I'm running out of patience here, Lou."

"I had an old prescription of Oxycodone in my medicine cabinet. There were only five pills left in the bottle so I told her to take one pill a night for a few nights to help her sleep. Months went by, and when my back acted up, I went to refill the prescription, but I was turned down because it had been refilled five times already. I confronted Sophia about it and she blew up at me, saying that she needed the pills more than I did."

"Are you telling me that you gave my daughter drugs right under my roof? You son of a bitch!" Trent yelled, punching the arms of his chair.

"I know I shouldn't have, but you had enough on your mind. I never imagined she'd take it as far as she did. I thought I was helping her. Then when you fired Vern, I realized you had given up all hope of finding her. I was losing my frigging mind so I got the hell out of your life. If she's not alive, it's as if I killed her with my own two hands." Lou broke down again, while pacing the room back and forth. "I have to get out of here!" he said, heading for the door.

"Lou, stop!" Trent said with his arms folded tight. "So you have been carrying all this guilt around for the past thirteen years? Of course I'm shocked, but I believe you never meant to hurt Sophia. I know you always loved her. Look at me," Trent whispered, clearing his throat. Lou twisted around to face him, continuing to keep a firm grip on the door knob. "I forgive you. I have to forgive you. Get over here, you old fart." The men hugged.

"Why don't you just sit down?"

"Just thought I'd point out that you look like hell, Vindigni."

"Thanks for noticing. I've been living in shit for a year, so some of it was bound to stick to me," Lou said, shrugging his shoulders.

"Do you have a job?"

"Does it *look* like I have a job?"

Both men really needed a good laugh.

"Wanna come back and work for me, like the good old days?"

"I'm not looking for charity, although it is obvious you could use some help around this place."

"It's not charity, and you know it. How would you like

taking orders from that woman? I'd better keep my voice down, I'm sure she has her ear pushed up to the door," Trent whispered.

"Thanks, Boss." The men shook on the agreement, and Lou went upstairs to clean up. His clothes were still hanging in his closet.

Gerda left in a huff the next day, swearing something in German while she packed her belongings

CHAPTER TWENTY-SEVEN

Lou was wheeling Trent into the dining room and said, "I don't know how you do it, Boss, all these therapists coming in and out at all hours, feels like Grand Central Station around here. Lunch is ready, by the way. You're not going to be taking your meals in the library anymore. You'll be sitting at the head of the dining room table from now on."

"You were right, things do taste better in here," Trent said, biting into his turkey sandwich. I'm finished with the sports section," he said, pushing the paper across the table.

"How do you think Mike Nolan is going to do with the Niners this year?"

He didn't respond. Lou asked again, knowing that Trent had always been a die-hard 49er fan.

"To tell you the truth, football doesn't rank high on my priority list anymore. The night of my mother's funeral I fell apart ... "

"I'm so sorry I didn't visit Rosa before she died. She was always like a mother to me."

"My mother knew you loved her, even if you couldn't always show it. What happened that night is nothing short of a miracle, and you know I have never been a religious man. I cursed God, can you imagine, right there in the church. And I know he heard me, because it felt like I was struck by lightning when I had the stroke right there on the altar. The doctors said that if that priest hadn't shown up right when he did, I'd have been dead within the hour. I see the world differently now. I'm just grateful to be alive."

"I know what you mean," Lou said, "I could tell something must have changed in you. I never thought in a million years you'd forgive me for giving Sophia those drugs. Speaking of miracles, I still believe Sophia could be out there. Have you thought about hiring another P.I.?"

"It's been too many years, there is no way she could still be alive. I am just grateful you came back, Lou.

Awkward silence filled the dining room. Lou pushed Trent's wheelchair to the library, and helped him back onto the recliner. It was time for his afternoon nap.

"Quit Mickey-Mousing around, go faster!" Trent shouted into the biting wind blowing in his face.

"What do you want from me? I'm not a machine you know. Once we reach the top of the hill I'll speed up, if that's all right with you," Lou shouted, straining to push the wheelchair. Trent leaned back laughing so hard he could barely catch his breath.

A couple of months earlier, Lou was surprised when Trent asked to be taken to Alta Plaza Park, a few blocks from the home. After the first week, Lou started packing lunches for them to eat there. Each day, they returned to their favorite redwood picnic table where they ate and played chess.

"Well, Lou, what do you say we invite people over for Thanksgiving this year?"

"I think it's a great idea."

"Great, do you have a piece of paper? I think we should make a list of who we want to invite, it's only a couple of months away."

"I agree," Lou said, taking paper and a pen out of his jacket pocket.

"Let's invite my sisters and their families, and how about Debbie and Colby?"

"I'll get to work on it right away. I miss seeing everyone, and I'm looking forward to preparing a real feast. I can't remember the last time we threw a party."

"Me neither. Colby and I passed the Bar Exam on the same day, it'll be good to see him again.

Lou was setting up the chess board while Trent watched a few small boys racing plastic trucks through a tunnel they had built in a nearby sandbox. He enjoyed watching the give and take of children learning how to work together. He was, however, getting a bit irritated by a child squealing in a high-pitched voice. Trent turned his wheelchair around, to see who was making all the racket. The toddler looked to be about three years old, and as she was being pushed high on the baby swing, she was half-laughing half-crying with excitement and fear. She screamed, "Higher, higher!"

The blond ponytailed babysitter seemed to be having as much fun as the child. The teenager turned around and looked straight at Trent. Her crystal blue eyes struck him with a familiar ferocity: She is Sophia ... she isn't... she wasn't ... she was ... his guts twisted. He felt like his head was going to explode. He could hardly take a breath, so he snapped his fingers trying to get Lou's attention.

"What's the matter?" Lou yelled, grabbing hold of Trent's shoulders.

"Get me out of here. Take me home ... I can't breathe!" Trent growled, pushing his fists against his chest.

Lou grabbed the handles of the wheelchair and pushed Trent as fast as he could, afraid he was having another stroke. "Hold on, I'm calling 911, just hold on!"

It wasn't another stroke, but after that event in the park, Trent flat out refused to leave the house anymore. He ate less, slept more, and cancelled all future visits from doctors and physical therapists.

The estate grew eerily quiet.

CHAPTER TWENTY-EIGHT

T wo years after her passing, Trent packed Alex's belongings and put them in a closet under the winding staircase in the downstairs hall. He couldn't bear to look at her clothes, jewelry, and other memorabilia, but he couldn't part with them either. Sophia's bedroom looked exactly as it had when she still lived at home, as if she would return any minute. Her door was kept closed. Just a glimpse of the stuffed animals crowded on her pink bedspread hit him hard with both hope and dread.

Lou opened the closet filled with Gucci suitcases and bags, neatly stacked. Opening up Alexandra's life again, hurt him more than he anticipated. While placing the suitcases back into the closet just as he had found them, he noticed a black leather attaché case leaning against the back wall. He sat down on the floor and leaning against the bannister, he gave into the temptation and picked the lock. Hesitantly, he started looking through years of birthday, anniversary and Christmas cards, and love letters Trent and Alex had written to each other. Reading the private thoughts of this happily married couple, Lou discovered a colorful love story. The handmade cards Sophia made for her parents were heart-warming. Her tiny handprints, forever present in plaster, touched his heart more than any of the other treasures.

He also found a few legal documents from Trent's il-
lustrious career as an attorney. In all ways, he had been a
successful man. Lou was saddened that his boss now sat
in a wheelchair, shutting himself away in a dark library.
A couple of hours passed before he carefully bundled the
treasures back together and placed them at the bottom of
the case. The tip of his index finger scraped the corner of
a small black book he hadn't seen beneath everything else.
It was an address book. He leisurely thumbed through the
alphabet, until he stopped short when he came across a
particular name and phone number under the letter J.

—————

Lou took the opened address book upstairs to his bedroom, closed the door, sat on his bed and dialed the phone.

"Hello. I am trying to reach a Mister David James. Is
this the right number?"

"Who may I say is calling?" a man on the other end
asked.

"My name is Lou Vindigni, and years ago I met..."

"Mister Vindigni, oh my God ... this is David. I have
tried to find you and Mister Martin for years ... I can't believe it's you."

"It's so good to hear your voice."

"We called his law office and spoke to Mister Hunt, but
he always refused to give us any information on how to
reach you and Mister Martin.

"Money can buy anything, so Trent made himself impossible to locate. Where are you living these days?"

"I live in San Mateo."

"I don't want to impose, but could we get together to
talk, maybe tomorrow?"

"Sure, I can get off work, where can we meet?"

"Why don't we meet in the lobby of the Marriott Hotel near the airport, let's say at two o'clock?"

"I'll be there, Mister Vindigni. Will Mister Martin be with you?"

"No, he won't. And please call me Lou."

———

When Lou walked into the hotel lobby the next day, David rushed up and gave him a huge bear hug.

"My God, man," Lou said, stepping back," it looks like you've grown another foot!"

"Lou, you haven't changed one bit. It's so damn good to see you, after what, twelve years?"

"Don't bullshit me, I've put on a lot of weight and it's all around here," Lou chuckled, patting his stomach.

They sat at a table next to the lobby-wide window facing the airport runway. A cocktail waitress brought drinks.

"Is Mister Martin alright? I was hoping to see him."

"I'll tell you all about what's going on, but first tell me what you've been up to all these years."

David explained that after graduating from Stanford, he became a Patent Attorney. He was now 32 years old with a wife and two children.

"I just thought of something ironic. My children are the same ages as my brother and sister were when you and Mister Martin found them."

"That's hard to wrap my mind around, and by the way, does Mama still work at the school?"

"Man, we really do have a lot to catch up on."

"I know we do, so how is she doing? Your mother has

always had a special place in my heart."

"You actually don't know what my mother does now. With all due respect, if you cared so much about her, why haven't you called to see how she is?"

"Every time I suggested that we go see *Mama's Arms,* or any of the other causes Trent supports, he's refused. He's never been the type who is comfortable with being praised."

"I am sorry, but we have been so frustrated. Mama and I even drove through Pacific Heights once, trying to pick out your house, but they all looked the same to us ..."

"I think it's time to fill you in on what's been going on since we last saw each other," Lou said, taking a deep breath.

Lou went on to tell him about Trent's life for the past twelve years, his deep depression from having never heard from Sophia again, the loss of his mother, and the crippling effects of his stroke. David was having a rough time digesting everything he was being told.

"Let's go for a walk," David suggested. "I need to get some fresh air."

The men went through the revolving doors leading out to the front of the hotel. It was 4:30, the wind was picking up as it usually does that time of day. They walked against the chill blowing off the bay, following a winding path parallel to the runway. Strong gusts prevented the men from talking without shouting to be heard. It was as if nature had provided the men with a much needed break.

David hadn't felt so small, so humbled, so blessed since Trent and Lou took him to find his family. He had just learned that Trent's life had changed radically, from being a man who only cared about making money, to one

129

who deeply cared for others. And that everything changed after that chance meeting with David on their flight back from Maui.

"Lou, can I go visit him?"

"I thought you'd never ask."

Chapter Twenty-Nine

L ou shouted, "This is the last time I'm going to say it, your bath is ready."

"Just leave me alone, can't you see I am trying to relax?" Trent shot back, jerking the foot-rest up on his recliner. "I've had it up to here with your nagging."

"You haven't had a bath in a week and you need a haircut. The barber will be here in an hour. And, yes, I made the appointment without telling you first."

Lou helped Trent into the wheelchair and pushed him to the bathroom. After the bath and haircut, Lou gave him chicken broth and crackers for lunch; the only food that tasted good to him anymore. Trent looked gaunt at 160 pounds on his 6' 4" frame.

It was 3 o'clock in the afternoon. The library doors were closed. The doorbell rang, and Lou opened the front door.

"You're right on time. I have no idea how he's going to react when he sees you," he said, patting David's shoulder.

"You didn't tell him I was coming?"

"I couldn't take the chance. He says no to everything these days, but Trent needs to see you even if he doesn't know it."

131

"Well, where is he? I'm as ready as I'll ever be," David said, shrugging his shoulders.

Lou opened the doors to the library.

"Wake up, Trent."

Trent opened his eyes and wiped the drool from the corners of his mouth with his sweater sleeve.

Usually in the late afternoon, bright sun streamed into the foyer through the stained glass windows on the front doors.

"Close the doors, the glare is hurting my eyes."

Lou walked out of the library.

"Mr. Martin, it's me."

Trent couldn't speak. The voice was familiar, ghostlike.

"It's me, David James," he said as he walked toward Trent, attempting to control the stream of tears coming down his cheeks.

"David, it's really you. Oh my God, son, you're a grown man." David was taken aback by how small and helpless Trent looked. Trent lifted both arms, like a small boy reaching for his mother to lift him.

David knelt down and the men hugged each other tight. Lou was watching the reunion from the doorway.

"Come on in here, you old goat," Trent waved Lou back into the room. "Is this why I had to get cleaned up today? Well, you son of a gun, you really pulled a fast one on me this time."

Lou prepared dinner while the other two got caught up on each other's lives.

"I would really love to see Dolores and the rest of your family. I am sorry I haven't reached out to all of you. Would you bring them over here for a visit some time?"

"I would rather take you and Lou to visit them."

"I'm really not up to going anywhere," Trent said, shaking his head.

"I'm sorry if I upset you, Mister Martin, of course I can bring my family to visit you here if that's what you want."

"Damn if you will," Lou called out, walking back into the library. "Look at it this way, you had a bath and a haircut today, so you won't offend Mama when she sees you. What day can we go see her, David?"

"Tomorrow would work for me, and I'd love to bring my wife and kids along with us. They haven't seen their grandma in a few weeks."

"Tomorrow will be perfect, right, Boss?" Lou asked, smiling.

"Fine, you win, I'll go. And by the way, is your mother still working at the grammar school?"

"We all have a lot to catch up on," David replied. How about we pick you up at one o'clock?"

"It sounds great, and we can all fit in the limo," Lou added.

David shook hands with the men and let himself out the front door.

"Lou, would you please pick out something decent for me to wear tomorrow?"

By 12:30 the next afternoon, the men were sitting outside the estate waiting for David and his family.

"I can't believe how long half an hour can feel," Trent commented while nervously shifting himself in the wheelchair.

"I know, and by the way, you look great in that suit, but it sure is obvious you haven't worn a tie in years. Here," he said, reaching over to fix the knot on Trent's tie. Trent shrugged Lou's hand away.

"I beg your pardon, I look quite dapper, if I do say so myself. Besides, you could have dressed up for the occasion."

"My shirt and slacks look just fine, you old snob."

"I hate the idea of David's family seeing me crippled-up. It just doesn't feel right, you know?"

"I think it's them turning the corner right now," Lou said, pointing down the street.

A silver Lincoln Continental pulled up to the curb. David's wife smiled through the passenger-side window, while the children giggled in the back seat.

"My goodness, David," Trent spoke up when the family stood in front of him, "I do believe this is the most handsome family I have ever seen."

"Thanks, Mister Martin," he replied, proudly smiling down at his children. "This is my wife, Dawn, and this is our four year old daughter, Riley, and my five year old son, Jack." Dawn gave both men a hug like she had known them forever.

Everyone got into the limo.

"Well, James family," Trent said, craning his head around to look at them, "where are we going? And another thing, please call me Trent."

"Okay, Trent, we're going to Oakland," Dawn said, smiling at her husband.

"I thought we were going to surprise Dolores at work," Lou commented.

"Actually the surprise is for the two of you, so just head toward the Bay Bridge and I'll direct you from there,"

David said, leaning forward to pat Trent on his shoulders.

"How old are Matthew and Briana now?" Trent asked.

They're fifteen and seventeen," Dawn answered. "They are great kids, I can tell you that. Mama has done a great job raising them, and of course David helps keep them on the straight and narrow," she added giving an affectionate squeeze to her husband's knee. The children started roughhousing in the back seat, so David separated them from elbowing each other. Their excitement demanded an outlet. Everyone in the limo, except Trent and Lou, knew about the surprise waiting for them. It was almost impossible for the four and five year olds to keep the secret. They laid their heads on their parents' laps, and eventually drifted off for a nap.

Trent wanted to learn more about Dawn, so she filled him in. Trent and Lou weren't strangers to her. Through the years she and her mother-in-law had talked about the men so often, she felt like she already knew them. Dawn, like her husband, had been a student at Stanford, and they met while studying in the university library. David graduated in 1994 with a degree in Economics, and she graduated the following year with a degree in Public Health and Safety, and subsequently got a lucrative job with the San Francisco Public Utilities Commission. They were married in 1996, and with the birth of their first child five years later, Dawn became a stay-at-home mom.

"Did it bother you to give up your career?" Trent inquired, feeling comfortable asking her.

"My decision to stay home came the instant we decided to start our family. I am blessed that my husband supports us so well. Few women have the choice nowadays," she continued, smiling down at her sleeping children. "Someday I will go back to work, or I might do volunteer work. I know you understand what it means to give without counting the cost, Trent. David told me, that 'til this day, you continue to help untold numbers of needy people."

"Hey, David," Trent said, turning around to look at him, "what kind of rumors have you been spreading about me to your beautiful wife? Don't believe everything that boy tells you, Dawn. The truth is I have lost my family and my health, so I'm ready to call it quits, but not today," he added, winking at her. "Let's just enjoy the day, but the truth is that, David, years ago you and your family changed my life, my outlook on people, and opened my heart. So I want to thank you. End of subject, folks."

———◦●◦———

"This area looks familiar," Trent remarked, leaning forward to get a better look at the street signs. "Didn't we go through the same area the night we met, David?"

"You have a good memory, we're almost there."

They arrived at their destination, that once had been a weed-covered park, scattered with sleeping bags, makeshift tents, and fire-pits that warmed its homeless occupants. The four square blocks had been bulldozed twelve years earlier, and out of the ashes Trent's dream arose. The men gasped. A neon-painted rainbow-shaped sign, hanging over the entrance to the mansion, spelled out:

Welcome To

Mama's Arms

CHAPTER THIRTY

The three-story mansion was surrounded by majestic oak trees, lush green lawns, with wild flowers covering the grounds. It was decorated with brightly painted murals of children running, climbing trees and doing cartwheels, with animals and birds somersaulting through blue skies.

Lou got the wheelchair out of the trunk, and after Trent was seated, David pushed him up the long red brick walkway leading to the entrance of the home, as Lou and the family followed behind.

Trent immediately caught sight of Dolores, looking like a statue at the entrance, her face beaming with pride as her son wheeled Trent towards her. Unable to hold herself back, she rushed to Trent and they embraced.

Lifting her chin to take a closer look, Trent exhaled, "Dolores, you are lovely."

She led everyone to her private office at the end of the long hall on the first floor. They passed numerous classrooms filled with children in grades K thru 8 working on lessons, doing artwork or playing musical instruments. The children's conduct was obviously held to a high standard. After sitting down in Dolores's office, two young mothers carried in trays of cookies, homemade muffins, ice water, tea and coffee.

"Thank you very much, Teri and Bette," Dolores said, introducing the women to Trent and Lou. It was apparent that everyone living there felt like family.

"Can we get you anything more, Mama?"

"No thank you, we're just fine. We'll join you later in the cafeteria, and would you please close the door when you leave? Thank you."

"Trent, what you have done, and continue to do, has already saved over a thousand lives. Since we opened our doors," Dolores continued, "seventy-five percent of those graduating after one year, have remained clean and sober and are gainfully employed. Most even come back as volunteers a couple of days a month. Through your endowment fund for extraordinary achievers, many of our high school graduates were given four-year scholarships to college. I can't tell you how much your visit means to us," Dolores said in a lowered voice.

She explained that after quitting her job at the Catholic grammar school, she became the head mistress and director of Mama's Arms. It was obvious to the board of directors, that she had a natural gift to inspire, delegate and manage the facility, so she was given the position. So for the past 10 years she continued to do everything in her power to make sure that Trent's original vision for the home was realized.

"Before I take you on the grand tour, how is your health, Trent?" David told me about your stroke. I am so sorry."

"I'm doing fine, I guess. As you can see, I can't walk anymore so I need these," Trent said, slapping the wheels on his chair.

"So why don't you tell Mama why it is you can't walk anymore," Lou quipped sarcastically, looking at Dolores like a kid trying to get his little brother in trouble.

"I can't walk because..."

"Before he starts feeding you a line of bull, I'll tell you why he can't walk. He refuses to keep up with his physical therapy. I've given up trying, maybe you can do something with this stubborn mule, Mama."

"Well, I'm not going to touch that one," she grinned. I think it's time to go on our tour."

She led the entourage past classrooms, offices, a workout facility, cafeteria, and the huge kitchen. They took an elevator to the second floor, and stopped at the chapel where a few mothers and children sat quietly in the pews. A statue of the Madonna and Child stood at the entryway, representing the heart of the home. Some upstairs classrooms were busy with mothers receiving adult education, while some of the high school students attended classes in another wing. Dolores led everyone back into the elevator and pushed the first floor button.

"Why aren't we going up to the third floor?" Trent asked on their way down.

"I'll take you up there later tonight. The housing units are on the third floor. Nobody goes up there during the daytime unless they are ill. I want you to be able to enjoy seeing the playground before it gets too cold outside."

"Good idea, Mama," David said putting an arm around his wife's shoulder.

A teacher was just leading a group of children outside for recess. David continued to push Trent's wheelchair, walking with a strut that resembled a victory march, while everyone else followed. The fenced-in grounds included state-of-the-art play equipment, basketball courts, and a baseball diamond. Trent was overwhelmed, seeing what was conceived at the fundraiser years before, had been achieved.

He noticed a peculiar sight at the far-eastern corner of the property ... a row of small wooden crosses lined up side by side.

Abruptly distracted, Trent motioned for Lou to come closer. "Excuse us, David, we need to talk privately for a minute."

"Did you see her?"

"What are you talking about?" Lou whispered, turning his back to the family.

"I swear that that little blond girl was a dead ringer for Sophia. She just ran past us."

"A herd of kids are running around, plus Sophia is thirty-three years old now, for God's sake. Get a grip. I'm not trying to be cold, but let's just enjoy the day. Let's finish the tour and then we'll go home."

You're right, today is about Dolores's family, and here I am turning into a blubbering idiot."

"I have to agree with you."

Dolores led everyone back into the home, although she had noticed Trent slumping a little sideways in his wheelchair. David pushed him to the entrance of the enormous cafeteria. Everyone stopped, stunned by what they saw inside. Over a hundred mothers, children, and teachers sat side by side at long dining room tables. Without saying a word, Dolores gave a signal, and all the children in the room stood up at their places. At the count of five, they turned to face Trent and Lou.

In a cappella, seventy-five children of all ages sang, "There's a Place for Us". It sounded like angels' voices echoing throughout the cafeteria. The men wiped away tears as they watched the smiling faces singing their little hearts out. The children had no idea the song had been the theme song for Trent's fundraiser, years before most of them were born.

"Dolores, you remembered," Trent said, reaching up to take her hand.

"Of course I remember. We sing it every Sunday morning in the chapel before the service begins."

"Are my eyes playing tricks on me?" Lou said a bit too loud. "It can't be Briana and Matthew. You two are all grown-up!"

David's sister and brother had taken a bus home from high school, and after a short talk about school and their extracurricular activities, they excused themselves to get started on their homework.

"Attention everybody," Dolores called out to everyone still in the cafeteria, "we're going to have pizza for dinner tonight!" The room erupted with shouting, clapping and the stomping of feet. Dolores had always said that pizza was junk food, and generally refused to allow it into the home. "Tonight we are going to celebrate," she shouted, clapping her hands in the air along with everyone else.

"Dolores," Trent said, "thank you so much for the great day, but I think it's time for Lou and me to head home. I'll send for a cab when David and the family are ready to leave, just have him call Lou, and we'll take care of it. I'm not used to getting out much anymore, and I think I might have overdone it today. I'm sorry for being such a party-pooper."

"Yes, I think it is time to leave," Lou agreed, "although pizza does sound super tempting."

"I have an idea," Dolores said. "Why don't you take a rest in our apartment upstairs and join us down here later? Everyone would be so disappointed if you left this early.

There will be plenty of pizza left over, don't worry," she continued, not giving Trent a chance to disagree. "And you wouldn't want to miss out on the special dessert we've ordered, would you?"

"You are one heck of a saleswoman, Dolores. You don't let up, do you?" Trent said, grinning.

"No, I don't. You wouldn't want to let the children down, would you?"

"Okay, you just closed the deal, Miss James."

"Lou, just take Trent to the third floor and go to room number 33...here are my keys," Dolores said, pulling them out of her dress pocket and placing them in Trent's hand.

When they arrived at the apartment, they were taken aback when seeing it still had the same furniture Trent had ordered for the family years before. It was clear that Dolores hadn't spent unnecessary money on her own family. Trent laid down on Matthew's twin-sized bed. They were touched to think that the 6 ft. 5 in., 17 year old high school basketball player still slept on it. He tucked the Spiderman bedspread under his chin and went to sleep.

"This is the best pizza I've ever tasted, Mama. I'm glad we stayed." Lou visited with the family at the end of one of the cafeteria tables.

"We're glad you did," Dawn said, while trying to get Jack and Riley to finish drinking their milk. "Tell us, how is Trent really doing?"

"He isn't doing well at all. Coming here today might just be the last time he agrees to go anywhere. He is very depressed, and being unable to walk has left him feeling totally powerless. To be honest, I don't think he wants to live much longer. Lately, he's been saying that he is anxious to see his wife, father and mother again. Thank you all for reminding him that his life hasn't been a failure. His daughter was the apple of his eye and I really don't think he can go on much longer without her.

Lou checked in on Trent a few times, and finally woke him up.

"I thought you'd never wake up."

"How embarrassing," he mumbled, wiping spittle from his cheek. "What time is it anyway?"

"It is 8 o'clock, and yes, there's still some pizza and lemon pie left over for you. It's lights-out in an hour, so most of the families are coming upstairs to get ready for bed now. Here, I brought you a cup of coffee."

"Thanks, you think of everything, but I'm not hungry, I just want to go home. Where's the family?"

"They are relaxing around the fireplace downstairs. It'll take me a week to fill you in on everything I learned while you were asleep."

"I just want you to know, and I'm only going to say this one time. I am damned proud to know you, Boss."

"I haven't done anything alone. You have been a huge part of all of it. After I'm gone, remember that. Now, help me get back on my wheels, Mister Vindigni. Let's call it a day."

CHAPTER THIRTY-ONE

L ou wheeled Trent into the hall. They stopped to make way for the stampede of children rushing to their rooms.

"The kids sure do make a racket," Lou said over the noise.

"Bedtime was always my favorite part of the day, Lou. Do you remember how I read books to Sophia every night while she snuggled under the covers with her stuffed animals?"

"I sure do."

"Alexandra always wanted to take part in the bed-time ritual, but I coveted it for myself. I was greedy with so many things. If I could go back, I would do so much differently."

Lou continued to push Trent at a snail's pace, taking time to look at the kids in the rooms.

"Trent," Lou whispered, pointing down the hall," is that the little girl you saw this afternoon? My God, she does look like Sophia."

"Yep, that's her alright. Seeing her felt like a kick in the gut."

The little girl, wearing pink flannel pajamas covered

with yellow butterflies, went into one of the rooms.

"It's definitely time to go home. I need a stiff drink, and we know there's no way to get one here," Lou yawned.

The doors of the elevator opened. Dolores and the family stepped out, waving.

"We almost gave up on you two," David chided.

"Mama, we can't thank you enough for such a wonderful day, but I think we're ready to leave. We still have a long ride ahead of us," Lou said.

David picked up his sleepy children in his arms and headed back towards the elevator.

"Daddy, I have to go potty," Jack whined, grabbing himself.

"Riley," Dawn asked, "do you have to go too?"

"Yes, Mommy."

"I'll take them," she whispered, lifting the children down.

Dolores had stopped at one of the bedrooms down the hall, and was quietly talking with a young mother. Trent turned in his chair to get a better look at what was going on. He was touched while observing Mama's demeanor ... so motherly as she spoke with the young woman with tenderness and respect. The mother's dirty-blond hair was pulled back into a ponytail. She folded her arms while intently listening to what Dolores was saying.

Responding to racket coming from inside the woman's room, Dolores asked the mother to remain in the hall, and excused herself.

"Children," Trent could hear Dolores's voice, "get under your covers and read your books quietly, please."

"Yes, Mama," their tiny voices replied, as Dolores returned to their mother.

Trent was mesmerized by her sensitivity with the young woman. She motioned, letting Trent know that she would join him in a few minutes.

"Take your time, we're not in a hurry," he mouthed back to her.

"Boss, let's get going, she'll understand."

"Dolores is doing what she does, and I want to wait for her. Why don't you go downstairs, I'm sure she'll be happy to take me down when she's done."

"I'll wait with you, Trent. It is amazing to watch what she has done with this place."

"It's my turn ... give it to me ... no, it's my turn," children could be heard arguing in the bedroom. The mother left Dolores to tend to her tired children, closing the door.

"Mama," a child called from a room further down the hall, "will you tuck me in bed tonight, pretty please?"

Dolores glanced over at the men, shrugging her shoulders and rolling her eyes with the 'what's a mother to do' look, before entering the child's room.

"Okay, young lady, but only one hug tonight, understand?"

"Do me a favor, would you, Lou? Roll me down to that room so I can see her with the children."

Stopping at the entrance to the room, they tried to be inconspicuous. A young mother was tucking her son and daughter into their bunk beds. Dolores sat on the edge of another bed, whispering a prayer with a little blond girl.

"Lou," Trent whispered, pulling on his sleeve, "there's the one that looks like my Sophia again."

"Amen ... now close your eyes and go to sleep," Dolores said, tucking the covers snug under the child.

Pushing herself up from the bed, she said goodnight to the mother and each of the children before leaving the room.

"Dolores, can I ask you a favor?" Trent asked.

"Sure you can."

"Would you mind if we say good-night to those children before we leave?"

Before going in, she knocked on the door to ask if they could go in just for a minute.

"Of course, Mama," the mother said, opening the door wide.

"Children," Dolores announced, "Mister Martin and Mister Vindigni would like to say goodnight to you, so please give him your full attention."

"What is your name, young man?" Trent asked the small dark haired boy with huge brown eyes.

"Jason."

"And how old are you, Jason?"

"I'm eight years old," the boy answered in a whisper.

"My name is Carmen and I'm five," his little sister chimed in, holding up five fingers and a wide smile which displayed two missing front teeth.

"Well, Carmen, I sure hope the tooth fairy gave you something special when your teeth came out," Trent said, smiling with her.

"Yes, she did. I got five quarters, and now I am very rich," Carmen giggled, clapping her hands.

"You sure are rich. The tooth fairy must think you are a very good little girl," he said, patting her head.

"And, what is your name?" Trent asked the blond, blue-eyed girl. She appeared withdrawn as she leaned against the headboard of her bed with her arms wrapped tight around her knees. She glanced at Trent with an expression of distrust.

"I bet I already know what your name is, honey."

"No, you don't!"

"I bet your name is Snoopy," he smiled.

"No way," the little girl giggled, shaking her head. Carmen and Jason ran across the room and began jumping on her bed, roaring with laughter.

"Her name isn't Snoopy," they shouted in unison.

"Carmen and Jason, get back in your beds right now," their mother ordered.

"Alright," Trent continued, "if your name isn't Snoopy, what is it?"

"It's *Alexandra.*"

———————

Lou clutched Trent's shoulder tight, and without hesitating, he swung the wheelchair around and rushed back into the hall.

Dolores hustled after them, worried that something was wrong."

"What's going on?" she said, tugging on Lou's arm. "Stop! Are you okay, Trent?" Dolores asked, stepping in front of him.

"Dolores, this is…"

"I'll do the talking," Lou interrupted. "Do you remember me telling you about Sophia, Trent's daughter who ran away?"

"Of course I remember. Did she come back?"

"No, she didn't, and that little blond girl in there looks exactly like she did twenty-five years ago."

"Oh my God, what did you say her name was?"

"It's Sophia," Trent said, "and I can't believe that little girl's name is Alexandra. That was my wife's name."

"Don't say another word," Dolores broke in, "we need to get to my office, now!"

CHAPTER THIRTY-TWO

D olores closed the door behind them and sat down. "Mama, what's going on?" Lou asked, feeling a chill shoot through his body.

"I think I might know your daughter, Trent," she said, choking up.

"What do you mean you might know her?"

"Just a minute, I need to get something. Don't move."

Dolores dialed her safe open and took out two sealed manila envelopes. She walked over and handed one to Trent. "I promised to give this to Alexandra when she turned eighteen, but I think you'd better take a look."

Trent ripped the envelope open, reached to the bottom, and pulled out a small black and white wrinkled photograph. He strained to look at the picture through the flood of tears blurring his vision. Lou went to stand behind him, so he could get a good look at it.

"Oh my God, it's your family."

The faded picture showed Alexandra, Sophia and Trent standing in front of the church, right after the seven-year-old received her First Communion. Sophia, wearing a white lace ankle-length communion dress and white veil, was being embraced by her parents.

"Where did you get this picture, Dolores?" he whispered with the photograph shaking in his hands.

"I am so sorry, Trent, Sophia's best friend gave it to me.

"Tell me where my daughter is!"

"If I cause you to have another stroke, I'll never forgive..."

"Just tell me the truth!" Trent screamed, his eyes bulging with tears.

"Okay, I'll tell you everything," Dolores said, slumping in her chair. "Seven months ago, two homeless mothers were brought here from Alameda. They were dirty, gaunt and ravaged by drugs, and their children were nothing but skin and bones. One of the women was Ruth Gomez, who you met upstairs with her children. She arrived with her friend, Sophia, and her six year old daughter, Alexandra. After a while Ruth and the children started to heal and put on weight, but your daughter's organs were already failing by the time she got here. She had Hepatitis C, which caused her liver and kidneys to fail. This is too hard, do you need something to drink?"

"I don't want anything," Trent said, laying his head back against the wheelchair headrest, staring straight up.

"I loved your daughter," Dolores whispered, wiping tears from her eyes. "Four months ago, I held her in my arms as she took her last breaths. I rocked her as if she were my very own. Sophia loved Alexandra with all her heart. Knowing that she was going to die broke her spirit with pain that can't be put into words. Sophia and Ruth were best friends, and she promised that after Sophia died, she would raise Alexandra with her own children."

"My daughter is dead!" Trent sobbed inconsolably.

Color finally returned to Trent's face. "Dolores, listen to me. Because of you, I know that my daughter didn't die alone and that she never forgot her family. She named her baby girl after her mother, and kept the picture of us with her all these years. I'm speechless. She never stopped loving us," he said, looking up at Lou.

"I have one more thing for you, Trent." She handed him the second envelope. "I am sorry."

He opened the envelope and tentatively unfolded a death certificate.

Name: <u>Sophia Rose Martin</u>　　*Died*: <u>April 16, 2006</u>
Sex: <u>Female</u>　<u>Unmarried</u>　*Age at death*: <u>32</u>
Cause of death: <u>Hepatitis C</u>　*Time of death*: <u>1:17 p.m.</u>

Trent could hardly breathe as he continued to stare at Sophia's death certificate.

"This can't be real ... it has to be a miracle ... I can't believe my eyes!" Trent gasped, almost choking on his words. "Listen ... Sophia passed away on the very same day my mother did. Look here." He turned the certificate for Dolores and Lou to see, poking at it with his finger. "Here, Sophia died on April 16th at 1:17 p.m. My mother said she could never die in peace until she saw Sophia again ... my whole family saw what happened. Listen to what I am saying. All at once my mother woke up from her coma and pointed to a corner on the ceiling of her hospital room ... she smiled and called out Sophia's name as she took her last breath. My mother died on April 16, 2006, at 6:32 p.m. Sophia had passed away only five hours earlier. My mother *did* see her granddaughter again, and my Sophia was there to welcome her grandma home."

"Oh my God in Heaven," Dolores rushed across the room to hug Trent.

"Where is my Sophia?"

Dolores escorted the men out to the far eastern corner of the playground, lighting the way with a flashlight. In the line-up of wooden crosses, was Sophia's, her name and date of death carved in bold letters. Trent couldn't stop the flood of tears pouring down his face. In dead silence they finally returned to the office.

After sitting for a few minutes, Lou broke the silence. "Trent, listen to me. If you hadn't found Dolores and her family all those years ago, and then built *Mama's Arms*, Sophia and little Alexandra would have died homeless. Can you comprehend what this means? You really did save your daughter's life. And right now there is a sweet little girl upstairs who desperately needs her Grandpa."

SIX MONTHS LATER

For the umpteenth time Alexandra whined, "Pretty please, Grandpa, can I open just one present tonight?"

"I'm going to catch you, young lady," Trent teased his granddaughter, chasing her around the Christmas tree again. "I'll get you with my cane," he joked, hobbling after her.

"Alexandra," Lou called from the kitchen, "help me get the cookies and milk ready for Santa Claus."

"Okay, Uncle Lou, I'm coming."

Never in the forty-two years since Trent purchased the estate did he have it decorated so magnificently as this Christmas. When carloads of families drove through Pacific Heights to look at the Victorian homes seasonally decorated, many lined up to take pictures of his. Spanning the roof, stood 50 seven-foot tall angels dressed in white while thousands of blinking white lights shaped like stars gave the illusion of earth rising to the heavens.

Trent stood looking out his front window, absorbing the beauty of lights on the Golden Gate Bridge, Palace of Fine Arts, Alcatraz and the Presidio. It had been many years since he had stopped long enough to enjoy the panoramic view of the city.

"Grandpa, are you okay?" Alexandra asked, tapping him on the arm.

"Oh yes, darling, I am just fine. Have you ever heard, "Twas the Night Before Christmas"?

"What's 'twas, Grandpa?"

"Oh, Alexandra," he chuckled, "come with me," he said, taking her by the hand into the library where ceiling-high book cases lined the walls. "Here," he said, taking down a large book of poetry, "would you please carry this for me?"

They walked back to the living room, and Trent sat on a large velveteen arm-chair next to the 20-foot Christmas tree. The many colored lights on the tree, playing off the silver tinsel, cast glowing orbs onto the peaceful manger scene nestled under the tree. Alexandra climbed up on his lap and he opened the book.

"Just a minute, go see if Uncle Lou wants to listen to the poem with us."

Lou joined them and settled down on the couch with a glass of red wine.

"Grandma and I used to read this poem to your mommy every Christmas Eve, Alexandra."

"You did?"

"Mm-hmm."

"Was Mommy a good girl like me?"

"She sure was. She was pretty like you, and she had a kind heart like you, too."

"Grandpa," Alexandra said with a big yawn, "I miss my Mommy."

"I know you do, Honey. I miss her too, I miss her very much."

"Twas the night before Christmas and all through the house..."

"Will you carry her up to bed, Lou?" Trent whispered, lifting Alexandra into his arms.

"Of course I will, I'm gonna call it a night too."

"I think I'll just stay down here and relax for a while."

"Just remember how early kids get up on Christmas morning ... and by the way," Lou asked, "what time are we going to see Dolores and the kids tomorrow?"

"I told her to expect us around 4. Did you remember to get all the presents wrapped?"

"Wrapped and already packed them in the trunk, Boss. Can't wait to catch up with everybody. See you in the morning."

"Good night, Lou. Merry Christmas."

Lou tucked Alexandra in her bed and turned off the hall lights.

"Merry Christmas, Boss," he whispered from the top of the stairs.

Trent dozed off in his chair. It was 4 a.m. when he woke up. He turned off the lights and headed up the stairs to go to bed. He couldn't make sense of the dream he'd had. Or was it a dream? Trent had been waltzing around the Christmas tree with his young bride, Alexandra, radiant in her wedding dress and veil ...then he was dancing with his mother when she was young, wearing a floral lace dress ... then he waltzed with Sophia, beaming in a flowing white gown.

Trent stopped halfway up the stairs and looked back down at the living room. He felt like he was still dancing, feeling lighter than air. The chill that covered his body contrasted with the warmth filling his soul.

He tip-toed into little Alexandra's bedroom and gently kissed her on the forehead.

"Merry Christmas, Honey, Merry Christmas."

ACKNOWLEDGEMENTS

Deep affection and sincerest gratitude goes to my family and friends who never stopped encouraging me to get this story out. And to Dawn Da Rosa, editorial and computer guru.

Special thanks to my three amigos, who continually inspire me with their love of writing ... while always exhibiting wild enthusiasm for my writing endeavors. For many years we have met for lunch at a Mexican restaurant, while being well-nourished by the spice we add to each other's writing projects. I thank Robert M. Davis (author of *The Ticker, Bum!* and *Will to Kill*) to Jana McBurney-Lin (author of *My Half of the Sky* and *Blossoms and Bayonets*) and to Martha Clark Scala (published author, poet, collage and video artist).

A very special thanks goes to my editor, Dave O'Shea, who also designed and illustrated the cover.

CPSIA information can be obtained at www.ICGtesting.com
Printed in the USA
BVOW08s1853010915

416096BV00001B/7/P